BLOOD PRICE

Cora's Choice – Book 6

V. M. BLACK

Aethereal Bonds
aetherealbonds.com

Swift River Media Group
Washington, D.C.

Copyright © 2014 V. M. Black

ISBN-13: 978-1501037214
ISBN-10: 1501037218

FICTION / General
FICTION / Coming of Age
FICTION / Fantasy / Urban
FICTION / Gothic
FICTION / Political
FICTION / Romance / General
FICTION / Romance / New Adult
FICTION / Romance / Paranormal
FICTION / Thrillers / Supernatural
FICTION / Thrillers / Political

In The Vampire's Presence

"I HAVE OTHER PLANS FOR TONIGHT." Dorian's expression left no doubt in my mind exactly what those plans entailed. My pulse quickened, my lips parting involuntarily.

His eyes narrowed at my reaction, a dark amusement in them that made my heart beat even faster. I shook my head at him, hoping that I looked disapproving. Everything still felt like too much, like the world was too real—the strange kind of spillover from Dorian's mood. This was something new, this direct, physical reaction to his moods, and it should have scared me, but instead, the force of it wound up my own brain until I felt like I had bottled lightning in my skull.

Definitely not a time for him to play teasing games in the back of his Bentley.

But also, I realized, definitely not a time that he could resist…even if I wanted him to.

Dorian's hand found my thigh, and a small spike of desire went through me, edged with the intensity that buzzed from him to me. He held my gaze as he slowly inched the hem of my skirt upward until his hand rested on the lace edge of the thigh-high. I shook my head again more vigorously, but my hand over his didn't try to push him away. Even my stockings itched now, setting my teeth on edge. He slid a finger under the top edge of the stocking, tracing a line across my bare flesh and leaving an irritated, tingling awareness in its wake.…

AETHEREAL BONDS

aetherealbonds.com

ACKNOWLEDGEMENTS

To CSM, who improves my books so much.

CONTENTS

CHAPTER ONE

I woke to the sound of the door shutting, and my questing fingers reached for the indentation next to me before my eyes even opened.

Empty. He was gone.

I was still grappling with the sudden, almost panicky pain of that when a voice cut through my thoughts.

"Good morning, Cora. Mr. Thorne sent me up."

I struggled out of the drift of pillows, pulling the blanket up with me as I straightened. Jane Worth was carrying a covered tray, and my stomach rumbled at the smells coming out from under it. She pretended not to notice that I was quite clearly naked, but she had a robe over one arm.

"Morning, Jane," I said, scrubbing sleep out of my

eyes with my free hand. I was disoriented for the brief-est moment by the navy and crimson room with the cold, impersonal decor that might have been in any exquisitely decorated hotel. Then I remembered that I was in Dorian's bedroom, not mine, and I remembered all that we had done the night before.

All that I had thought….

I love you. I'd almost said those words aloud. To him. A vampire that I thought I'd do anything to escape. The vampire I still hoped to escape.

Didn't I?

What was wrong with me?

"Where's Dorian?" I asked instead.

"Mr. Thorne is working this morning but will join you this afternoon."

I suppressed a twinge of…something. Fear? Relief? Disappointment?

I had hoped that after the night before….

I didn't really know what I had hoped, except that I wished I had woken with him again.

"Is he here? In the house?" I asked.

"I couldn't say," Jane replied, carrying the tray across the room.

Of course, whatever he said that I meant to him, I was only a small part of his full life, one that was crowd-ed with demands far more important than any merely personal claim. He had his businesses to manage and his research to oversee, never mind his role among the machinations of the various vampire factions, against the Kyrioi who believed they should rule men and in support of the Adelphoi who believed vampires should live alongside them.

I had a full life, too—one waiting for me back at campus. I was only a semester away from my economics degree, and I'd just received the acceptance to my top pick of grad schools. And I had a boyfriend, an honest-to-goodness human boyfriend, who was funny and sweet and respectful and pretty much everything I should have wanted.

And yet here I was, waking up in a vampire's bed, in his world, where my life must, by necessity, revolve around him. All because I had been among the small minority of humans to survive the blood-kiss of a vampire. The transformation that had followed had both cured my terminal leukemia and bonded me to him for life. I rubbed my inner wrist where the mark of our bond stood out, scarlet against my pale flesh, as if there were an answer there, imprinted on my skin.

Jane set the tray on the table where Dorian and I had eaten dinner the night before. It had been cleared, I noticed, while I was sleeping. The clothing that had littered the floor was also gone.

Exactly how many people had been through here while I was sleeping?

"Your robe," Jane said, coming to the side of the bed and spreading it so that I could turn my back to her and slip into the arms, keeping up a pretense of modesty.

I did so, wrapping myself in the thick terrycloth as I slipped out of bed and tied the fat belt, taking the opportunity to survey the room. The one set aside for me was next door to it, a study in neutrals in contrast to the rich colors of this room. But this room didn't look much more lived in than mine had when I'd first arrived. Everything looked designed, planned, the mark of the decorator much stronger than that of the person—the agnate, as vampires called themselves—who inhabited it. The books on the shelves had been chosen for the colors of their spines, and the baubles could have been from any magazine. But more striking than what was present was what was absent. There were no photographs, nothing imperfect or out of place, no objects at all of a recognizably personal nature. It looked more like a set than a bedroom.

I found that vaguely sad.

Sitting at the table, I raised the lid of the breakfast tray. Fruit blintzes, eggs benedict, some kind of savory French toast, bacon and sausage, hash browns, and a fizzy sort of juice cocktail to drink. Once again, I wondered if the chef had any expectations that I'd finish it all. I hoped not, because it was enough for four of me.

Jane had retreated to stand against the wall in a kind of modified parade rest. She still had a slightly pinched expression on her face. I'd unintentionally insulted her—multiple times, actually, with a complete lack of social grace—and she hadn't forgiven me for it.

I'd ignored her hurt feelings because I'd viewed any kind of relationship with her as no more than temporary. I'd been determined to find a way to escape my bond to Dorian, even if his every touch set my body on fire, even if his gaze seemed to be able to see my soul. He wanted too much of me—he'd change too much of me.

Now…. Now, I wasn't sure about anything.

"Look, Jane," I said, my fork suspended in midair, "if you're going to be my lady's maid, you can't hate me."

Jane's face spasmed in horror. "I don't hate you, m—Cora!"

"Then why the—" I almost said *attitude*, but I caught myself just in time. Yeah, insulting her again would be a great way to reach an understanding. "Why don't you seem happy?"

"You disapprove of me and of my work," she said, staring fixedly at the opposite wall.

"No, I don't," I said. Then I winced as I went through the catalogue of my interactions with her in my mind. I'd refused the wardrobe she had selected for me except when I absolutely had to wear something other than what I owned. I'd brought my own toiletries without commenting on her selections. I'd even insisted on hauling my own luggage up to the room.

Right.

I set down my fork. This was going to take some work.

CHAPTER TWO

"I'm sorry," I said. "Look, none of it was about you or what you've done. It's just that I woke up here, after the change, and I was told that I had a new life when I already liked the one I'd had before. Dorian wants to give me all these things, and a lot of them are wonderful, overwhelming, even. But they're too much."

"They're your due as his cognate, madam," Jane said frostily.

I sighed. "That's just it. I know you've been waiting years for a cognate to show up—that's your job, after all—but no one consulted me about…about any of it. I didn't exactly read a contract and sign on the dotted line. I just woke up, and I was here with all this waiting for me." I gestured to indicate my rooms, my wardrobe, the entire house.

Jane still didn't meet my eyes. "Any woman would consider herself lucky to be in your place."

"No, she wouldn't, because I don't." I took a breath, telling myself that jumping down her throat wasn't helping the situation. "I didn't. You work here, and you see all that a cognate gets, and maybe you're even a little jealous. But you don't think about how much she has to give up—how much *I* have to give up. I've got another life, and it's real, and it's as important as anything. That's the life I wanted to save, not this one. This one belongs to someone else. It's been waiting for someone to swallow up since before I was born. And if I let it do that to me, then I didn't really save my life at all."

"Don't you love him?" Jane demanded, sounding horrified. "You have to love him, though. You're his cognate. You have to be his cognate, and you have to love him."

I rubbed my forehead. Did I love him? Last night, I had thought that I did. Dorian was icily remote, terribly controlled, but beneath that was a fire that burned so brightly I feared it would consume me. And that was mixed with his peculiar tenderness and consideration, and finally, under everything, that sadness, that deep well of grief that I could hardly touch.... I felt that I would give anything to wipe away that sadness, even though I sensed that I was, already, part of its cause.

Was that love? I didn't know, but I was very much afraid that I couldn't live without him anymore, with or without the bond.

But how could I accept it, if it meant that I'd never truly be free?

"I don't know," I said finally, heavily.

Disappointment flashed across Jane's face.

"As you say, madam," she murmured.

"God, Jane," I snapped. I couldn't deal with this, but I knew who could. Lisette, my best friend, was never at a loss for words. I knew just what she'd say. "I can't be your imaginary dream cognate. I am who I am, okay? And I can't—I won't just throw myself away to make you or anyone else happy."

"I don't want you to make me happy," Jane blurted. "I want to make you happy. That's my job. Don't you like your room? It may be too bland, I know, but I couldn't know what you'd like."

"I like the room just fine," I said.

Jane didn't seem reassured. "And you've hardly touched the clothes I picked for you except when you've had to. I really did try to get a wide selection because the clothes you came in were, well, very neutral in style."

"The wardrobe was amazing." I realized that we were already getting far off track. "Look, everything you've picked out is great. But it's not mine. And you're, well…." Oh, God, now I was dancing on the edge of a knife blade. I spoke carefully. "Dorian's the one who arranged for me to have a lady's maid. I've never had any servants or staff or anything like it, and it wouldn't even have occurred to me to ask for a maid, not in a hundred lifetimes. It's weird, okay?"

Jane's face froze. "I fail to follow."

Open mouth, insert foot. Okay, time to try again. "I mean it's weird for me. Not weird, period. You've had the idea that you'd be my lady's maid for years. I've had the idea that I'd have one for less than a week."

She nodded fractionally, her eyebrows drawing together as she considered that. It was a start.

"You didn't just become the perfect lady's maid overnight, right?" I nudged.

She relaxed a little, her expression brightening. Who says flattery doesn't work? "No, Cora. I've been working for years, always studying, keeping abreast of the latest fashions, and all that."

"Right," I said encouragingly. "Well, I think maybe being a...mistress takes practice, too." I almost choked on the word. I didn't know yet that I was going to be her mistress even a week longer, but I wouldn't tell her that. "And I don't have any. Practice, I mean. So please, just give me some leeway here, some benefit of the doubt. I'm trying to do right by everyone."

The mask over her face slipped a little more. "I guess I forget that you haven't studied all the same books that I have."

"Exactly." I decided whether I should press my temporary and unaccustomed advantage, and I decided to go for broke. "Maybe a lady's maid is a friend, and maybe not, but you should at least be my ally."

Jane looked startled, then stricken. "I'm sorry, Cora. I do want to be your ally. I just feel that you're working against your own best interests. Against your heart."

Of course she did. How else could she feel? She was in Dorian's thrall. She would die at his word. "I know you feel that, Jane. You and Dorian both. I'm sure that we'll work out something in time." *If we have the time*, a little voice whispered in the back of my head. "Until then, I need you and all the rest of the staff here to not hate me."

Jane looked scandalized. "Oh, we never would."

"Right, then," I said, hoping that she meant it. "So then—relax a little. Sit down." I pointed to the chair across from me.

Jane instantly went rigid. "I don't think that's quite proper."

"You're supposed to be working for me, right?" I said. "Well, I can tell you right now that I'm absolutely not proper, and as long as you keep hoping that I will be, you'll be disappointed. So now that we've gotten that out of the way, *sit*. You make me nervous, standing over me."

Jane crossed to the table and sat. Then, abruptly, all the remaining stiffness went out of her frame as if a barrier had been broken.

"I'll still let you do my makeup and tell me what to wear, okay?" I promised. "Just don't make me feel like I'm living in *Downton Abbey*. Seriously, I'd be no good at that."

Jane cracked a smile. "Yes, Cora."

"Have you had breakfast? Eat some of mine. I'm sure I'm letting down the chef every time I send back a platter more than half-full."

She eyed the tray. "I've eaten already."

"Then at least have a piece of bacon."

I held the plate out toward her, and she stared at it for a long moment. Finally, almost as if it were against her will, she plucked a single piece off the top and nibbled it fastidiously.

"There, now," I said, hoping that my bossing had done some good and I hadn't just bullied a maid for no reason.

I dug into the cooling breakfast. The food tasted every bit as good as it looked. Jane still seemed at least moderately thawed, so I chalked up my first victory: Cora, 1; Dorian Thorne's staff, 100. Or something like that.

"How exactly did you come to work for Dorian?" I asked after a moment of silence. "Did you answer an ad? 'Ageless vampire seeking staff. Please apply only if adaptable to a Victorian lifestyle and undisturbed by the occasional puddle of blood.'"

I couldn't help but see the parallels between Jane's situation and my own. But I'd been forced into my arrangement with him—the bond that was formed when he first drank my blood had cured me of my terminal cancer even as it had sealed me to him as his consort.

Like all those who worked for Dorian, she was under a lesser kind of hold, a thrall, created when she consumed a tiny amount of her own blood mixed externally with his. This increased the agnate's influence on a human so that he could control them even outside his presence by placing a compulsion on her to think and act a certain way.

I couldn't quite handle the idea that someone would give someone else that power willingly without the kind of stakes that I had faced.

Jane finished the bacon and wiped her fingers carefully on a spare napkin. "My parents were in service," she said. "When I was old enough, I chose to join them. The old lady's maid was retiring, and there was a big competition for the position, but I won it in the end."

"So...did you go to school? Like—" I was about to say *a regular person*, but I stopped myself and took a quick swallow of juice to cover my near-slip.

Jane's lips twitched as if she were trying very hard not to smile. "Yes. My parents own a house in Gaithersburg, and I went to school there. Back then, of course, not quite as many girls went to college, but Mr. Thorne has demanded high standards of his lady's maids forever, and even the one who was retiring had a home economics degree. So I applied at sixteen for the scholarship, you know, so I could take all the fashion, design, hospitality, and family and consumer sciences courses at the university."

"What do you mean, *back then?*" I asked, a bit of blintz dangling on my fork. Jane only looked slightly older than I was.

"I graduated from high school in eighty-three," she explained.

I looked at her again. No, it wasn't possible—not even Hollywood stars managed to age that gracefully. "Okay, so what part am I missing about this going-into-service thing?" I asked. "Dorian said something about a thrall slowing aging somewhat, but that much?"

At that, she did smile. "It's dependent on how often the thrall is renewed. One of Mr. Thorne's researchers has been studying it in his spare time. We don't heal as fast as you do, and we're not as strong, and we have only slightly more resistance than regular humans to things like colds and the flu, but the slowed aging is considered one of the biggest perks of the position."

"And that's worth it to you? To let him into your head?" I pressed.

"Mr. Thorne only uses the thrall to ensure that we are perfectly loyal," she said stiffly. "But of course, I would be, anyway, so mainly his thrall means that other agnates won't try to corrupt us very often."

"Like the one who caught you in the Best Buy parking lot did," I said.

"Right," she agreed, her face clouding. She'd been forced to betray me under the involuntary thrall of one of Dorian's enemies, causing an assassin to be sent after me. "That hardly ever happens these days since everyone knows it will be discovered in a few weeks at the most when the original vampire's thrall is renewed. But if Mr. Thorne didn't use a thrall, all of us would constantly be in danger of other agnates pressing us into their service as spies."

"And what happened to you was...different from Dorian's thrall?" I was afraid that I was pushing a sore point, but she had nearly gotten me killed.

"When it's something you wouldn't want to do normally, it's like a hand around your brain, making you think other things. It feels...wrong," she explained, casting her eyes down at the breakfast tray.

That was very different from my bond. My bond always felt right—no matter how alien the urge.

I shivered. It was time to think about something else.

"So by choosing Dorian's thrall, you're under only a few obligations, you get the whole long-life angle, and you are mostly left alone by other agnates," I summarized, keeping my tone bright as I cut a piece off a sausage. "Is that about right?"

"That's it," she agreed. "For me, it just means that I would never, ever tell anyone who shouldn't know what he is, for instance—not that I would anyway. And maybe I work a little harder at my job or like it a little more. I don't know. But the pay is good and the hours, though irregular now that you're here, aren't long. And I love it. I love my job. Not many people can say that, but everyone who works for Mr. Thorne can."

"Hmm," I said, taking another bite of French toast. It didn't sound that great to me, to give someone unbridled access to your mind, even if they promised not to use it...except to make you perfectly loyal, of course, and to like working for them more. At the same time, though, I couldn't deny that the deal must seem attractive to many, especially if all the people you knew best lived much longer than ordinary humans. Not going into service would then seem like contracting a life-shortening disease, like Huntington's or muscular dystrophy.

"Anyway, it's important that no one talks to ordinary people about what Mr. Thorne is, even accidentally. They can become very unhappy when they believe there is an agnate in their midst," Jane added.

"Pitchforks? Torches?" I joked.

"More or less," Jane said. "And then people get killed for no reason."

As opposed to being killed to slake the agnate's thirst. It was a fine distinction, I thought cynically, but that didn't mean she didn't have a point.

"What if you want to quit your job and work for someone else? Or do something else?" I asked.

"Oh, I never would, but if I did, he'd let me go," she assured me. "When people want to retire or take off for a few years or stay home with their kids. He even lets us continue the thrall, if we want, even though we're not working for him, so we still get the benefits."

And he still got their loyalty. "How kind of him."

Jane stood then. "Now, if you don't need anything more, I need to prepare your clothing for your outing this afternoon," she said.

"Outing?" I repeated.

"Yes, the yacht party," she said, as if that were an explanation. "I'll just be in your dressing room when you're ready."

Oh. Dorian's New Year's Eve party was on a yacht, was it? I had just assumed that it'd be another gathering somewhere in his cavernous house.

I finished the breakfast and took a shower before surrendering myself to Jane's mercies again. I thought, very briefly, about insisting that I wear my own clothes, but I knew that would effectively erase any progress we'd made toward reaching an understanding. And anyhow, I had no doubt that anything that I'd brought with me would look ridiculous at one of Dorian's parties.

A winter daytime yacht party seemed to call for a calf-length, buff-colored wool skirt, a cowl-necked cashmere sweater, subtly beaded, and a matching blue-gray cloche. She explained that the merino pea coat would be waiting for me downstairs. Thigh-high seamed stockings—for warmth, Jane explained—and kitten heels finished the look.

Then Jane applied a thick layer of sunblock to every exposed bit of skin.

"You will be outside part of the time, after all," she said judiciously.

Fortunately, my manicure was still declared to be adequate, and the time that went into my hair and makeup was less than half as long as the night of my introduction. With my light brown hair in a finger-wave updo, I decided the entire look had a distinctly *Great Gatsby*-like vibe.

"Beautiful work, Jane. I guess I'm as ready as I'll ever be," I said, surveying the woman who looked almost like me in the mirror.

Ready to face down Dorian's vampire guests. Again.

But this time, I wasn't under his compulsion. I wasn't shaking in my shoes. Instead, I was standing there of my own free will—or as free as it could ever be as long as the bond remained. And I was preparing to meet his friends as equals, to judge what course my future would take, whether to join them or to break away forever.

Because that could still be my choice—my fatal, final choice that once made could never be undone, for if he drank my blood again after the bond was broken, it would cost us both our lives.

CHAPTER THREE

I emerged from the dressing room carrying my purse and hat to discover Dorian lounging in one of the armchairs near the window, a laptop on his knee. His broad forehead was creased in a slight frown as he tapped at the keyboard, his sharp blue eyes fixed on the screen and his mouth pressed in a line of concentration.

Working. Working on part of his life that was outside of his relationship with me.

If I chose him, could I have the same?

He flipped the screen shut when he saw me and stood, setting the laptop aside. "Good afternoon, Cora."

Damn, but he looked good—today in camel-colored pants, a lighter jacket, and a dress shirt with a textured brown silk tie. As always, not a single black hair on his head was out of place, and he exuded aristocratic wealth and elegance. I wondered how many years it would take for me to look like I belonged at his side.

Probably never, I decided. Hopefully never, because if I looked like I belonged with him, I wouldn't look like myself.

His eyes raked across me, hungry as always and shadowed with the memories of what we had done the night before. His body on mine, in mine, his mouth everywhere at once....

I cleared my throat.

"Is it past noon already?" I asked. I was usually an early riser.

"Jane came up with the tray at ten," he said. "So yes, it is."

"Oh."

"Are you ready to go?" he asked. Leaving the laptop, he crossed to the door that led onto the mezzanine.

"Why not?" I said. *No* was definitely not the answer he was looking for.

And, I realized, it wasn't the one I wanted to give.

Why did I suddenly feel so invincible? Dorian could obliterate my mind with little more than a thought, stripping away absolutely everything that was me. I knew this. I'd felt his will upon me before—I always felt it as an undercurrent, behind vast walls of restraint. Walls that could be broken.

But he hadn't destroyed me yet, and though one day he might, either in a moment of wrath or a slow erosion of my very self, he wouldn't do it today. And today I could choose my tomorrow.

Dorian waved me through the doorway and offered his arm, one of his peculiarly outdated mannerisms that seemed perfectly natural coming from him. I took it with my free hand, the thrill of touching him going through me. And I wasn't invincible anymore. I was small and frail—not frightened, not exactly, but at the very edge of fear, knowing what strength was beside me.

There was so much I wanted to say as we walked down the mezzanine corridor, so much that crowded in my brain and my throat. Just two days before, I'd learned that I could break the bond between us if I slept with a human man, and I'd almost done it, almost claimed my freedom and my old life.

I was half-certain he already knew, but I wanted to tell him myself what I'd almost done with Geoff. I wanted to explain how badly I'd wanted to be free of the demands he put on my body and my mind. How badly I still wanted it.

And how I still couldn't let him go. Not then. But maybe, maybe later....

But I couldn't say any of it. And yet the energy of those words, of the elaborate dance I had placed us in, seemed to sizzle between us.

"Do you ever get tired of dressing up all the time?" I asked instead.

"Dressing up?" He raised an eyebrow, his expression so bland that I knew that he was teasing me right back. His steps, always so measured, had a restless kind of energy in them. If he were anyone else, I would call it a nervous excitement.

I looked askance at him. "Your three-piece suits.

And your oxford cloth shirts. And your smoking jacket, for goodness' sake."

"I was at the office when I came to get you yesterday," he pointed out as we reached the head of the stairs. "And today, we're going to a party."

"You wear a three-piece suit to work."

"One must look one's best. It's a good way to put others off their ease."

Another joke. He was in an unusual mood today, and the sense of restrained impatience seemed to zing off him. I could feel it spilling over, onto me. My breath came faster, my step hitching a little as I matched his quicker one, the echoes of our footsteps too loud and the texture of the sweater against my skin suddenly almost intolerable irritation.

"I don't think you need fancy clothes to help you do that," I said as we started down the arching marble flight. "Do you dress up for dinner, too?"

"Of course," he said.

"Every night?" I pressed. "Even when you're alone?"

"Unless my routine has been disrupted, yes," he said, looking bemused.

"I hope you don't expect me to do that," I said. "I've got better things to do than change clothes for a meal."

"I consider that to be a negotiable point," he said, the corners of his eyes crinkling with humor even as he kept his tone flat. "If we have guests?"

"I'll dress then," I granted him.

"And if we go out?"

"Okay, depending on where we're going, I'll change clothes for that, too," I said.

"Then I'm satisfied."

"I'm not," I said as we reached the landing. "Do you have clothes that aren't suits? Or dress shirts and blazers?"

"At the moment, not many," he admitted, stopping as he pivoted around the corner, the hub to my wheel.

"Then go buy some. Or have your maid or whoever do it for you. It actually is okay to relax sometimes."

"So you want to change me." The words were light, so light that it was almost possible to miss the barb in them.

Almost.

Suddenly, I had the sensation of having two conversations at once: one a frothy banter, the other deadly serious.

I narrowed my eyes at him. Dorian was looking ahead, down the stairs as we took them together, but I could feel the tension in his body—and the darkness in his mind.

"You've already changed me," I said, carefully matching his tone. "There should be some kind of balance. So that means that you need to do some changing, too."

"And my wardrobe is of the greatest concern to you?" he asked, again the sharpness of daggers hidden in the words.

"It's a start," I said.

"That sounds ominous." A joke again—and a question, because he was tossing back at me much of what I had said to him.

"It should," I agreed.

He wasn't going to talk about what I had almost done with Geoff, I realized then, however much he knew or guessed. That was too dangerous for either of us. Instead, we were having this not-conversation, this almost-conversation, shying away, glancing near, and never quite touching home.

I was grateful, because if anything could break the walls around his will….

His answer broke into my thoughts. "I'll notify my valet of the changes he should make."

And that was his concession and also his acknowledgement of my need for control, for an influence over him, however voluntary it was on his part.

And however involuntary the changes he made in me.

His step had neither faltered nor slowed, as if we were talking about nothing at all, and we soon reached the front door, where we were met by the butler and two uniformed maids who held our outerwear.

I shrugged into my jacket, accepting the help of the butler, then set my hat on my head and took the sunglasses and scarf from the maid with a murmured, "Thanks."

The first time Dorian's staff had helped me at the door, I'd felt exquisitely self-conscious. Now it almost seemed, if not normal, at least appropriate. The thought was a little chilling that I could ever get used to something so foreign from my old life—my real life.

I looked up at Dorian. He had put on a dark brown

pea coat over his blazer. With his hat and aviators, attention was drawn away from his piercing eyes, and my gaze was drawn irresistibly down to his sensuous mouth and long jaw.

That mouth. Oh, God.

I still didn't feel at ease with him. Not really. But when I looked at him now, there was a piece of my soul that seemed to light up in recognition. With belonging.

The butler opened the front door, and I winced involuntarily against the burst of light even with the protection of the sunglasses. The courtyard was frosted in two inches of fresh snow that must have fallen the night before, but the paths were already swept clear. At the curb, the Bentley waited, warm and purring, with the chauffeur standing ready to open the rear passenger door.

"Not driving yourself?" I asked as I swung into my seat, still feeling the effects of the strange energy that seemed to push him on.

"Not today," Dorian said before the door shut.

I wriggled out of my coat, pulled off my sunglasses, and sank into the leather's warm embrace. Even Dorian's cars were seductive. As I buckled up, Dorian settled into the seat next to mine, and the chauffeur got behind the wheel.

"So, an afternoon yacht party," I said as the Bentley pulled away from the curb. "I assumed that a New Year's Eve party would start at nine or ten at night and run into the next morning."

Dorian glanced over at me. "I have other plans for tonight."

His expression left no doubt in my mind exactly what those plans entailed. My pulse quickened, my lips parting involuntarily.

His eyes narrowed at my reaction, a dark amusement in them that made my heart beat even faster. I shook my head at him, hoping that I looked disapproving. Everything still felt like too much, like the world was too real—the strange kind of spillover from Dorian's mood. This was something new, this direct, physical reaction to his moods, and it should have scared me, but instead, the force of it wound up my own brain until I felt like I had bottled lightning in my skull.

Definitely not a time for him to play teasing games in the back of his Bentley.

But also, I realized, definitely not a time that he could resist…even if I wanted him to.

Dorian's hand found my thigh, and a small spike of desire went through me, edged with the intensity that buzzed from him to me. He held my gaze as he slowly inched the hem of my skirt upward until his hand rested on the lace edge of the thigh-high. I shook my head again more vigorously, but my hand over his didn't try to push him away. Even my stockings itched now, setting my teeth on edge. He slid a finger under the top edge of the stocking, tracing a line across my bare flesh and leaving an irritated, tingling awareness in its wake.

I bit my lip and I cast a look at the chauffeur, but he didn't seem to notice what was going on in the backseat—or was at least well-trained enough to feign ignorance.

Dorian did nothing more for a long time, his tracing fingers working back and forth across my thigh until I thought I would scream. My legs were slick with my need, the hot smell of sex filling the small cabin. But I could neither urge him on nor make him stop. I seemed trapped in the moment, the frustration of it, as it wound tighter and tighter inside me.

I could watch him, though, watch his beautiful, predatory face. The face of a killer. Of my angel. I could watch the smile curve those sensuous lips, those icy blue eyes locking with mine under the black wings of his brows as he watched what he was doing to me and drank it up.

My hand tightened over his as he slid it higher until it met the elastic edge of my panties. He hooked one finger under it, traced up and down the crease of my inner thigh, chafing against the damp skin. My heart was beating wildly now, skittering out of control, and I felt the heat build between my legs, weeping with my need for him. My center, my legs, my clit—they all ached for him. I hated and loved it at the same time, forcing myself to hold still, to not tilt into his hand in invitation. I couldn't wait for the torture to end—but I wouldn't take one step to end it.

His fingers slid farther under the damp fabric, and I caught my breath as he teased along my folds, my hand tightening around his wrist until my knuckles went white. *Oh, please,* I thought. *Please, please, now, please, don't—*

I didn't even know what I wanted to ask for. I didn't have words for it. The energy crackled off me, from my body to his and back, until it almost hurt.

And then without warning, he slid one finger deep inside as his thumb found my clitoris.

I bucked forward against the seatbelt and I cut off a gasp, closing my eyes against the wall of sensation that surged out from his touch. I felt my entire body clench around him, concentrated around his touch inside me, warring with the irritating gusts of heated air and the scraping of my clothes' seams and the against my skin. Everything but him was unbearable. And the only relief was him.

He slid in a second finger beside the first and began to move them. I looked down to see my skirt, tumbled up into my lap, and his wrist emerging from under its edge. From between my thighs. My brain almost could not take it in, the sight of him under my skirt and the feel of him inside me. I felt his darkness then, the seething power of it, sliding out from him to touch my raw brain—oh, God, not to change me but to do something so that, for a moment, I was a part of the darkness, too.

I wanted to come. I wanted to come so hard that I would scream my throat hoarse. I reached for the climax, clawed for it. I didn't care about the driver in the car anymore. At that moment, I wouldn't have cared if I were in front of an audience of thousands. But Dorian matched me perfectly, and every time I got close, he tore my satisfaction away, stilling or speeding or shifting his hands until my fingernails dug deep, angry marks into his skin.

The car stopped, and all at once, Dorian pulled away, and I was left, gasping, desperate, and bereft.

"We're here," he said softly.

The words hardly registered. My gaze rose to his face, trying to wring some sense from them, and then I looked beyond him, out his window to see a forest of masts against the sky. A marina. We were in the heart of the District, just steps away from the edge of the Potomac, and we were also at a marina.

Dorian opened his door, and the sudden blast of daylight shook some semblance of reason back into my head. Flustered, I slid on my sunglasses and fumbled with my buckle and coat. The chauffeur was at my door by the time I got my coat buttoned, and I stepped on wobbling legs out into the brilliant afternoon light.

"This way," Dorian said, offering me his arm as if nothing had passed between us—except for the tension in his body, striking a harmonic that made mine hum in sympathy.

Why? I wanted to ask. What was this new thing between us; what was he trying to do to me, and why? Was he punishing me? If he'd wanted that, surely he would have done it the night before. Was he punishing himself? Or was he nothing more than a vessel for the buzzing, saw-edged energy?

Not knowing what else to do, I took his arm, aching and frustrated as he led me down a sidewalk toward the boat slips, every step chafing the swollen sensation between my legs.

Even in my befuddled state, I knew immediately which boat must be his. It was at the end of a dock and was easily twice the size of any of the others—a huge white yacht that towered over the gray marina.

"You really don't do many things by halves, do you?" I said as we began walking between the neat white lines of sailboats and day cruisers toward the monstrosity at the end.

I spoke more acerbically than I'd meant to. But he'd teased me into a pitch of arousal that I couldn't even articulate.

"That's not something we agnates are known for," Dorian returned, an edge in his voice that matched what I felt.

To go all the way, to the heights that only he could propel me from where I was now…I could hardly imagine it even as I wanted nothing more.

The gangway was already down, and we were greeted at the top by a young man—well, I corrected, thinking of my conversation with Jane earlier that day, a young-*looking* man—in a white uniform who offered us flutes of champagne. Dorian plucked one up, but I passed. I would rather face a group of strange agnates stone-cold sober, I decided.

"Your guests are in the salon, Mr. Thorne, Ms. Shaw," the man said.

"Thank you," Dorian said.

"Are we late?" I whispered as we walked along the deck. I looked back to see the gangway being pulled up behind us.

"Not at all," Dorian said. "They knew when we would be arriving. We'll meet them in a moment. But first—"

He opened a door and pulled me in with him, hitting the light as the door shut behind us. It was a small utility closet, a mop and bucket leaning against the wall.

"What—?" I started.

But he had already turned me to face him, plucking off my sunglasses and setting them on a shelf with his and the champagne flute before pinning me against the door and lifting my skirt to yank my panties down, his hand sliding between my legs again as his mouth came down over mine. My purse dropped nervelessly from my fingers.

I knew what was coming, I craved it, but the feeling of his fingers plunging deep inside me was still shocking. It ripped a whimper from my throat, and I gave it to him, gladly, gave my surrender to his mouth that covered mine. It had to end, this torture that rasped across my nerves. I was so swollen with need that when he slid a third finger in, next to the other two, I felt like I would break from the fullness. Still he pushed me to the edge, to the edge and not over. And I didn't know whether I was going to die or kill him.

Knocking off his hat, I grabbed his hair and pulled his mouth down harder against mine, giving myself to him utterly even as I demanded every bit of him in return. And he obliged, his lips against mine, his tongue deep in my mouth, his fingers inside me, moving, stroking.

And then he let me come, and the force of it almost took me away, my mind bobbing in its riptide. My brain went, my knees went, my body seemed to fly apart even inside its skin. And he pulled back even as I was still shattered, and I cried out again as his fingers slid out of me, leaving a swollen emptiness, a hollow fullness in their wake. He caught my wrists together in his hand that was wet from me, pinning them above my head against the door as I struggled to make my legs and feet and knees work together as they should to support me.

"As you said, I'm not much for half measures," he said, laughter in his voice as he loosened his belt and fly. It was a sharp, ragged laughter, a cutting one, and it made me shudder again.

He jerked my panties off, tearing them, and I couldn't even think a protest as I finally managed to make my legs support me again. But only for the moment, because he lifted me up against the door, his hands boosting me up under my thighs so my legs wrapped around his waist, opening me to him completely.

But I was the one who reached down, who guided his cock to my most vulnerable parts, who welcomed the thick length of him into me until our pelvises met.

"Kiss me," I begged. "Kiss me again."

Dorian did as I throbbed around him, wild with the feel of him inside me, needing his mouth, his lips, his tongue, which stroked me until I wished I would die from it.

Then he began to move, thrusting into me, pushing me mercilessly against the door. And all I wanted was more, closer to the place where pleasure edged into pain, until that buzzing irritation was obliterated in the sheer physicality of his body driving into mine.

There was no finesse to it. It was fast and hard and dirty, and my center twisted and tightened until it tore and dropped me into the hot embrace of the climax that rippled down through my aching clitoris into my center and pounded up into my head. He held me then, pushing me deeper into the heat of it, until I thought I would come apart.

Until all I wanted was to come apart.

Just as the last echoes left me, his frame gave a great shudder, and he came, too, deep inside of me as I panted against his shoulder. Slowly, he lowered me to the floor, then took a cloth handkerchief from his pocket and kissed me again, gently, as he used it between my legs to remove what he had left there.

"Cora, if you had any idea—" The words came out in a fast, rasping whisper, almost tumbling over one another until he bit off the last one. They were still rough, hard, despite the tenderness of his touch.

I just sagged against his shoulder, my mind blank, my body still throbbing with his contact. He'd branded me, just like I'd been afraid of all along. Branded my sex. Branded my soul.

What had just happened? How had it happened? I was standing there in the mop closet with a vampire, still Cora Shaw, but somehow not the same. Not ever the same.

Dorian straightened and folded up the handkerchief before making it disappear back into his pocket. He stooped and retrieved my panties and handed them to me. But they were now torn, useless.

"You're rough on lingerie," I observed, managing to find my voice. It was still my voice, saying the sorts of things I would say. "Really, on all kinds of clothes."

He took the panties back and dropped them into

the mop bucket. "I can get you more."

"Yes, but right now, I don't have any," I pointed out.

He flashed that smile again, that peculiar, edged one that was almost manic. "A bonus."

Right. I straightened my clothing as best as I could, exquisitely aware of the fabric of the skirt against my naked rear. I replaced my sunglasses and tried to check the position of my hat by feel, but as Dorian opened the door onto the deck, I had the sinking sensation that the evidence of what we had done would still be written on our faces.

I cast a glance at Dorian, who was sipping his champagne as if nothing had happened.

Well, at least my face, then.

Damn him.

CHAPTER FOUR

D orian opened another door, and I discovered
that the salon was a large living area decorated
in pale sand colors along severe modern lines,
the perimeter surrounded by tinted windows that looked
out over the Potomac on three sides.

There was a small group gathered there, agnatic
power palpable among them, and I froze in the doorway
as the men in the room stood up. Smoothly, Dorian
took my arm and led me inside, and I took a deep
breath and squared my shoulders next to him.

No more cowering. No more quaking. Whatever
happened, I was done with that.

A woman in a steward's white uniform stepped
forward to take our outerwear, and I surrendered my
coat, hat, sunglasses, and purse.

"Ladies, gentlemen," Dorian said, ushering me
forward, "Allow me to present Cora Shaw. You all met

at least briefly at her Lesser Introduction, but I doubt that many lasting impressions were made at the time."

Ten. There were ten guests in the room, five men and five women, and at a swift assessment, I decided that they were divided evenly between agnates and cognates.

Dorian was, I realized, making an effort to introduce me to other couples. His friends, I supposed. The first vampire party I'd attended had been a big society affair, to which every agnate in the region had to be invited or risk a mortal insult. Dorian had warned me then explicitly that not all the agnates would be like him—and how right he had been. I'd seen things that night that still frightened me.

This handpicked group must be the kinds of relationships between agnate and cognate that he wanted me to see. And they seemed, from the carefully open smiles that a few of them wore, to be determined to make a good impression.

I recognized only two of the guests: Jean and his cognate Hattie. Hattie worked for Dorian in his research lab, and she'd been the doctor in attendance when Dorian had bitten me and caused my conversion and bond. I'd met her again at the first party I'd attended, along with Jean, who'd seemed to treat her with indulgent condescension.

Dorian made quick introductions. Will and Elizabeth, Dalton and Marie, Raymond and Francisca, Jean and Hattie, Oleg and Svetlana. I nodded to each and tried very hard to match names to faces, but I was pretty sure I had all but Jean and Hattie mixed up almost immediately.

"Pleased to meet you," I said stiffly, feeling that something was expected of me.

"Oh, likewise," said a red-haired agnatic woman with a smile that was probably meant to put me at my ease.

"Good to see you again, Cora," Hattie added warmly.

"Indeed," said Jean, sounding bored.

Dorian guided me toward a sleek fawn loveseat, and I tugged at the edge of my sweater before perching on the edge, my legs clamped together self-consciously.

Hi, everyone. Nice to meet you. I'm not wearing any underwear, I thought.

As soon as I sat, all the men in the room took their own seats, agnate and cognate alike. Dorian settled next to me, taking my hand between his own.

I realized then that I had an answer to a question I'd wondered about some time before: Dorian's old-fashioned manners were that of a gentleman to a lady, not an agnate to a cognate.

I filed away that piece of information for later, when I could decipher what it meant or even if it mattered.

A tiny cognate with olive skin and waist-length jet black hair exchanged a meaningful look with her agnate before turning to me with a bright smile.

"You are a student, I heard? At the University of Maryland?"

I glanced at Dorian, but his expression was unreadable.

Then I chided myself. I didn't need his permission or reassurance to speak.

"Yes," I said, lifting my chin. Then, in hopes that I didn't appear curt, I volunteered, "I'm studying economics."

"Oh, yes!" the long-haired cognate said. "What a fascinating field it is. So many changes! New ideas, new models, but it does seem that economists never can agree on anything."

"As they say, when you put two economists together, you get three opinions," I joked weakly.

The sound of the yacht's motors increased, and out of the windows, I could see the dock slip slowly away.

The red-haired agnatic woman chuckled. "As long as the twin beauties of diversification and compound interest continue to work, I'm happy enough and don't care if I never learn more."

"That's because you are a sybarite," her cognate teased affectionately. "You only care about what directly impacts your own physical comfort."

She shrugged, accepting the charge.

"So, what do all of you do?" I said, for lack of anything else to ask.

"We are most of us idle rich," said a blonde agnate in a thick Russian accent. That would be Svetlana, I thought, retrieving the name.

"Some of us are more idle than others," an agnatic man said dryly. "Portfolio management can take a fair amount of time. And, of course, there's the scheming. We spend a great deal of time scheming."

"But Hattie works. Doesn't she?" I asked, casting a

look between her and her agnate Jean. "I mean, he lets you work?"

"Oh, most definitely." Hattie smiled at him as he lounged against the cushions of their loveseat. "I had my doubts, but Jean insisted, certain that I'd love it. You see, I was studying chemistry when we met, but chemistry was a very different science so long ago, and I didn't know how much help I could be."

"But after just a few years of study, she had become the most indispensable member of our team," Dorian put in.

"With all the hours she puts in, sometimes I wonder whose cognate she is, after all." Even Jean's grumble was tinged with ennui.

Hattie rolled her eyes at him. "That's not something you're likely to forget any time soon. And Will works with us, too."

She nodded to the cognate who had called the redheaded agnate a sybarite, and he shrugged.

"When Elizabeth chooses to spare me," he said.

They were all so comfortable with each other and with their world. I wondered how many years they had known each other. Fifty? One hundred? Longer? They were trying so hard to make me feel welcome that it made me even more self-conscious that I didn't fit in with them.

Couples. Every one of them. Unbearably beautiful people, monsters and angels. And Dorian and I....

I looked around, trying to see us in one of the pairs of guests, not sure whether I was more afraid that I would or wouldn't.

A parade of white-uniformed stewards appeared then, bearing trays upon which a variety of tantalizing refreshments were laid out. I welcomed the interruption. I wasn't used to being the focus of the room, much less a room full of vampires and their consorts. I was always the "and"—Lisette and Cora; Geoff and Cora; Hannah, Sarah, and Cora.

Everyone loaded small plates, and a bartender took orders for cocktails and champagne before retreating to a bar in the corner to prepare them. I watched the guests as they selected their delicacies. Their movements were almost like a dance. I realized suddenly when I'd seen something like it—in a documentary I'd watched once about geishas in Kyoto. They had the same grace. But with the agnates and their cognates, there was nothing that seemed contrived about it. The habits of movement had been ingrained untold years ago.

I smiled politely as the first steward reached me and picked a few of the most delectable-looking appetizers. Each of my movements seemed clumsy and awkward in comparison to the balletic elegance the others gave even the slightest motion, and in my self-consciousness, I tried to hold as still as possible.

"Now that you know your research works, you should come away for a while," Jean was saying to Dorian. "Take a vacation. You haven't been to the Riviera since it was full of Russian noblemen. Rhodesia, Brazil, Tibet—you used to be so much fun."

"It's Zimbabwe now, not Rhodesia," Dorian said dryly. "And this is only the beginning of our research. I'm sure Hattie's been filling your ears with it all."

Jean shook his head. "Most likely. But I never listen to her when she talks shop. It's so dull."

Hattie gave him an unsubtle pinch, and he smiled indulgently down at her.

"I'm saving the world, and he acts like I have an orchid obsession or I'm into stamp collecting," she complained, but her eyes twinkled with suppressed humor.

"Jean, you pay attention," Svetlana chided gently. "Is important."

"One-in-one-hundred is significant. It's the magic number that makes our side far more attractive than that of the Kyrioi," Dorian said. "But it's only the beginning."

"As long as we control the technology," Elizabeth said shrewdly. "Are you sure your labs are secure?"

"The laboratory is inside Dorian's house, and we prove every worker weekly," Hattie said in a tone that said they'd rehearsed this argument many times before. "Every phone and computer belonging to any of them is bugged. Every home, too. I don't know what more we can do."

"We've foiled three attempts since Cora's introduction," Dorian said. "But you are correct. The Kyrioi probably will eventually gain control of the technology, too, likely within five hundred years. Not even the silkworm was kept a secret forever. We must use the time until they do to persuade more people to our cause."

"Hearts and minds," Svetlana's cognate said.

"Indeed," Dorian agreed. He looked over at me.

"But we didn't come here to discuss such weighty matters."

"Every conversation with you turns into a weighty matter," the long-haired cognate said, nestling against the side of her agnate. He hushed her, and she gave him an impish smile. "Señor," she murmured at him and subsided.

The third male agnate shot his cognate a significant look. They had both been silent so far. The green-eyed woman looked back at him for a long moment before turning a timid gaze my way.

"Are you from the area?" she asked. Her voice was so soft it was almost a whisper.

"Yes, I'm from Glen Burnie," I said. "That's where my grandmother raised me."

"It's such a…lovely area," the cognate attempted.

"Oh, Marie, you could at least try to sound convincing," the long-haired cognate broke in.

"No, it's quite all right," I said. "It's not a great part of the state, but it's not downtown Baltimore, either."

The stewards returned to collect the plates and wineglasses, and then a man entered in hospital scrubs, pushing a cart loaded with medical-looking supplies.

"Oh, Dorian, you never can just enjoy yourself, can you?" said Jean, rolling his eyes. "Every time you get us together, it's research, research, research."

Dorian spread his hands. "You know we're out of samples again. We seem to be near another breakthrough—we just need a little more."

"Now that you have your own cognate, I hope you don't suck her dry," said Marie's agnate.

Svetlana waved gracefully. "Keep watch on Dorian, Cora. He's prone to bit of...hyper-focus."

The long-haired cognate looked up at her agnate through her eyelashes. "Why don't you all run along? Keep you away from temptation."

Because of the blood, I realized, remembering Dorian's reaction to my blood on another occasion.

Elizabeth chuckled throatily. "Wish to keep the gathering rated PG?"

"We are supposed to be welcoming Cora, not frightening her, and having you drool over me while I'm getting blood drawn is not the way to do that," Will said crisply.

"We're going," said Dorian. Standing, he looked down at me and explained. "The phlebotomist is collecting blood for my research. You don't have to participate if you don't care to."

I shrugged. At this point, it was hard to get too worked up about a needle. "I've donated blood before. I guess this is for a worthy cause, too."

His lips curved. "The worthiest."

I watched Dorian lead the rest of the agnates from the room as the phlebotomist approached the first of the consorts.

"Well, that got rid of them," the long-haired cognate said. "I'm Francisca, by the way, in case you missed it. But everyone calls me Paquita. My other half is Raymond." She flopped against the back of the sofa with a kind of gamine unsophistication that was, I decided, entirely conscious, pushing up her sleeve to bare the crook of her arm.

I wondered if it had to do with how long the agnates and cognates lived, that they had enough time to decide not only how old they wanted to be but how they smiled, how they walked, how they waved their hands. Or maybe it was just because so many of them came from an age when posture and deportment was drilled into middle and upper classes from birth. Either way, I wondered if they were now capable of a genuinely graceless movement.

"I have heard all about you, of course," Paquita said as the phlebotomist set up a blood collection bag and inserted and taped the needle on her arm. "It's probably rather unnerving to have everyone you meet already know your background, but your conversion is such a milestone for all of us."

"Dorian said that it's a justification of his research," I said.

"Oh, certainly, and more—it is the first conversion to ever be studied with any scientific accuracy. The data that was collected could really be a breakthrough." She laughed. "Of course, that's more Hattie's domain than mine." She nodded to the blonde cognate, who was already lying back as well.

"Dorian didn't tell me that his research team included cognates," I said. "Before we met, I mean." It occurred to me for the first time that maybe Dorian's offer to give me one of his businesses to run was more than just a bribe meant to buy my acceptance of our bond. If Hattie had a vocation in addition to her position as Jean's cognate, perhaps he really meant for me to lead one of his ventures, not just pretend to be the

CEO.

"Don't let Dorian fool you," Hattie said. "He likes to play at the amateur gentleman or wealthy patron, but he gets his hands dirty, too. He's unusual among agnates. So few of them ever make anything at all. The first few years, he barely stopped to eat or sleep. He was a man possessed."

"I can imagine," I said. And I could. It fit neatly into my growing picture of him—a driven man who clung to his scruples, haunted by old angers and old griefs. The rising demon....

I realized that every person in that room likely knew more of Dorian than I did, despite our bond. I had met him not even six weeks before, but Hattie and probably several of the others had known him before I was born.

It was an unsettling thought. I was closer to Dorian than I ever had been to any human in so many ways, and yet he was still so much a stranger to me. A phrase from somewhere came swimming out of my mind: *The past is a foreign country.* Dorian's past spanned empires, and I could never visit there. No matter how well I came to know him, there would be parts of him that remained far beyond my reach.

The phlebotomist moved to Hattie's side as Paquita's collection bag slowly filled with blood.

"You probably didn't get all our names the first time," Hattie said then, perhaps misinterpreting my silence for shyness. She went around the circle again, and with the three women now clear in my mind, I only had to assign Oleg's name to his long face.

"How are you handling it?" Will asked. He was the only one other than Svetlana who bore a recognizable accent, an upper class British drawl. "The conversion, I mean."

"It's been very...strange," I admitted.

I thought of my desire and fear, my struggle to keep myself intact and my driving attraction to Dorian that had somehow turned into something more. I didn't know how to put any of it into words, not even with these people, who should be able to understand if anyone could.

The cognates were looking at me expectantly, so I continued. "As I'm sure you've heard, I agreed to a medical procedure because I was terminally ill. Dorian...well, you know...and I woke up nearly a week later to realize that I'd just been bitten by a vampire and turned into...something else," I finished lamely. "I don't hardly even know him, still, and I don't know what I feel about everything—what I should feel about it."

The phlebotomist moved on to Will, who just rolled up his sleeve without bothering to lie down like Paquita and Hattie had.

"You mean you don't know if you should love him. Oh, you spoiled modern children," Paquita said, smiling at me affectionately. "For me, conversion was a gift from the Holy Mother, nothing less. I never deluded myself that I would choose the man I was to marry."

Hattie made a slightly offended clicking sound, but Paquita ignored her.

"I was terrified that it would be old Bermudo Barrientes, who would give me saucy looks every time my ama took me to church," Paquita continued. "Raymond was young and handsome—which Señor Barrientes most certainly was not. And Raymond didn't have foul breath or indigestion. And he was kind and generous beyond every expectation. And most of all...he loved me, and I could love him. I wasn't afraid of whether I *should* love him. He is my husband. Of course I should love him. I was afraid that I would be married to someone I couldn't love."

"It was easier for you, Paquita. You're a woman," said Oleg with cheerful chauvinism. I wondered why his agnate had such a heavy accent when he did not. "Now me... I was in a carriage accident. Leg crushed, turned to gangrene, not expected to survive. This amazing woman comes to the room in the inn where I'm put up, and the next thing I know—well, there are certain things you don't think you'd be doing at death's door with a crushed leg, but let me tell you, I do my best. I wake up days later, and my bachelor life was over. It's in the worst taste to be devoted to one's wife, and yet I found myself driven to satisfy her—and only her. It was a shock to my system, as the phrase now goes."

The phlebotomist approached Marie.

"But you were okay with it?" I asked. "I mean, with her changing you?"

Oleg shrugged. "Well, I would not say that it was easy at first. And she had to keep the chambermaids away from me for a year or two. But I realized that I was happy with her, and that's what really matters."

"But are you really happy?" I asked. "Or is she just making you think that you are? She could erase your mind, twist your desires, change who you are inside."

Marie cleared her throat, and everyone turned to look at her. She was a slender, pale woman with a froth of red-gold hair, as insubstantial-looking as her soft voice. "I was married before…before Dalton. It was not a happy union. Any husband could beat me, insult me, practically imprison me, if he were so inclined. How could I hope to challenge a man's strength?"

Her liquid eyes were dark with remembered pain. "When I was young, a husband would have the strength of law behind him, too, to do most of those things. But just because Dalton could do terrible things to me doesn't mean that he will. There are good agnates and bad ones, just like human men. I have a good one, so I don't concern myself with what he is capable of. I care about what he actually does, and he is good and true."

The room went silent, and Marie dropped her gaze to the spot just above the crook of her arm, where a bond-mark in the shape of a tiny, lopsided heart lay.

The phlebotomist was at my side now. I rolled up my sleeve, half-stunned by Marie's words. I had never really considered what Geoff was capable of doing to me if he wanted to. I knew he wasn't abusive, so I'd hardly considered that his athletic height meant that he could hurt or kill me, and I would be defenseless against him. It just wasn't something that I worried about, because I knew it wasn't in his nature.

So why did I fear Dorian? Was that any less far-fetched, really?

Except that I could sense the darkness in Dorian, could feel how badly he wanted to change me—and I knew how much easier it would be if he did. Geoff could hardly accidentally beat me, but Dorian was capable of making profound changes while not even fully recognizing what he had done. Dorian always seemed to be at the edge of the night, while Geoff stood squarely, safely in the sunlight.

I winced and looked away as the needle slid in. The phlebotomist taped it and moved on to Oleg.

"So none of you ever wanted to break the bond," I said, risking the words.

"Well, I told you about the chambermaids," Oleg said, waggling his bushy eyebrows suggestively. "But that was long ago."

"No," said Paquita firmly.

Marie shook her head.

"No," said Will. "I would not commit adultery for any reason, much less to be free of a bond that is no burden to me."

"I would not be faithless," Hattie agreed.

I looked at them all, feeling painfully alone. "You could be human again, couldn't you? Live a normal life. And nothing would happen to your agnates, would it?"

"A normal life would have had me making babies for Señor Barrientes until I was old and fat," Paquita said. "And I would have died many years ago."

"There is much happiness I never would have seen. Besides, he is my husband, and a good one. Why would I throw all that away?" Marie asked in her small voice.

"But he really isn't your husband," I said. "I mean, you weren't married."

"Some of us are," said Will. He held up his left

hand, displaying the ring on his finger. "And those who aren't—well, 'husband' and 'wife' are the human terms, so they still do well enough."

I shrugged uncomfortably. I certainly didn't feel married. Bonded—yes, that I definitely felt, far more keenly than to my liking. But it was a world away from what I imagined when I thought of the word marriage. I had always expected an egalitarian relationship, the kind that most of my friends' parents had and I imagined my Gramma and grandfather, my mother and father had enjoyed, too.

But this—there was never any doubt in this relationship where the power lay. The bond was both more complete and more terrible than I ever imagined a marriage could be, a true joining that blurred my edges while his remained bright and distinct. If two people had become one, it was perfectly clear that the "one" would have to be him.

I watched the collection bag fill slowly with blood and wondered how many of those cognates could even make the decision to break their bond—how many were left with the ability to want to. And if they couldn't, was it really love? Or was their contentment merely a reflection of what their agnates wanted them to feel?

Was there ever an end to the circle?

"Have other cognates done it?" I asked. "Broken the bond, I mean."

Hattie and Paquita exchanged long looks.

"There was Sarah," Hattie said after a moment. "She was married when she was converted. She had children, too, young ones. And she wouldn't give them up. Like you, she had been dying—tuberculosis, which wasn't treatable back then—but she returned home the moment she had a chance and pulled her husband into their bed...and that was it. She gave it all up."

"And there was Johann Bauer, too," Oleg put in. "Two hundred years, he'd had, and then, when he was as drunk as a pig, for a moment's lust for a bit of skirt at a tavern.... I don't know whether Madeline was more devastated or infuriated by his betrayal."

"It happens," Marie put in. "Not often, but it happens."

"Do they regret it?" I asked.

"It hardly matters if they do," said Will. "Once converted and returned to humanity, there is no going back again."

But it did matter. I needed to know. Had Sarah cried over her agnate? Or had she rejoiced to be free of him and his demands?

But the cognates had grown frosty with my questions, and I didn't want to push any harder, so I led the conversation to a safe topic—other boats they had traveled on at other times—and the cognates relaxed again.

After the collection bags had been filled and taken away, the agnates rejoined us, and everyone wrapped up against the cold and scattered across the deck of the yacht, going through permutations of conversational groupings to the backdrop of the shores of the Potomac. I watched the groups change and noticed how the couples seemed to gravitate back towards one another, connecting, if only for a moment, before shifting into new social constellations.

I stayed at Dorian's side. I couldn't tear myself away. My thoughts of bonds and breaking them had frightened me again, reminding me how close I'd come to doing just that. Even though I still wasn't sure that breaking the bond wasn't exactly what I wanted to do, any thought of losing Dorian was like a physical pain only his presence could soothe.

Did I fear losing him only because the bond was still in place? Or would something of what I felt now linger, a canker of regret, for the rest of my life?

Or did it even matter how I would feel if breaking the bond meant giving up so much, here and now?

From the rail, I watched D.C. slip by—all the hurry and bustle and intensity of the capital seeming at once very immediate and far removed from the lazy progress of the yacht on the river. The afternoon turned to evening, and the shapes of the buildings grew more shadowy as the lights began to twinkle on the shore. The sunglasses came off the guests' faces all around the deck, and lights strung on the railing and various parts of the superstructure of the ship came on. Music began to play, and I looked up a stair to the upper deck to see a band there, under a canopy of tiny lights. More hors d'oeuvres were passed on silver trays, and the drinks flowed freely.

I'd been too distracted to notice when we turned around, but several hours after dusk had drawn on, we arrived back at the dock and the gangway was lowered.

I looked up at Dorian. "That's the party?"

It certainly seemed understated for a vampire bash,

not that I had much to compare it to.

"Oh, no, it's just beginning," he said. "But we are going somewhere else."

He took my unresisting arm and wrapped it over his. The cold air already frosted from our breath and bit at my nose and cheeks, and it was still hours before midnight. As long as our destination was warmer than the open river, I wasn't going to protest.

"So you're ditching your own party?" I prompted, walking with him down the gangway to the dock.

"I have a more important place to go," he said. "And even though these guests are my friends and allies, I don't think you'll enjoy an evening among even more strangers."

As we headed up the dock toward the parking lot, we passed several knots of revelers going the other way, toward the yacht. Several of them had the unmistakable agnatic force around them, but most did not.

One group, already tipsy, roared out a greeting to Dorian. He raised a gloved hand in acknowledgement.

"They're not vampires," I whispered after they had passed.

Dorian looked amused. "Whatever made you think that they all would be?"

At that, I was somewhat stumped. "Well, only agnates and cognates came to my introduction."

"That was different. This party is one of the premier New Year's Eve social occasions in the city. People fight tooth and nail for invitations. Agnates, senators, lobbyists and various hangers-on, captains of industry—you'll find them all here."

I had a sudden suspicion. "And how many of them are under your thrall?"

The corner of his lip twitched. "Before tonight or after?"

I shuddered. "That's not a funny joke."

"Who said I was joking?"

"Where are we going, then?" I asked, changing the subject as we reached the parking lot. "Home?"

He smiled down at me. "You'll see."

A familiar low-slung yellow car rolled up, interrupting my retort. The driver's **door** opened before I could react, and Cosimo stepped out, sporting a flamboyant designer suit.

"Ah, Dorian, Cora, my dear," he said.

My hand tightened reflexively on Dorian's arm. At least his awful cognate Lucretia was nowhere in sight. She and Cosimo had tried to scare me into breaking the bond with Dorian and so discredit him.

But whatever I chose, it wouldn't be because of them. I could only choose what was best for me, for my own life. Whatever meaning others chose to attach to it was not a concern of mine.

"I don't remember your name on the guest list," Dorian said coldly.

"Oh, if I waited for invitations from you...." Cosimo waved airily. "I was so looking forward to the evening with you. But it looks like you aren't staying. What a shame."

"Isn't it?" Dorian said, walking right past him to where his Bentley idled, waiting for us. I held too hard to his arm. "Good evening, Cosimo."

"Good night," Cosimo called out after us.

I looked back. He was smiling. I didn't like that at all.

CHAPTER FIVE

The chauffeur pulled out of the parking lot, turning onto the street with no orders from Dorian.

"One side has to win, Cora," Dorian said quietly. "The Kyrioi or the Adelphoi. Perhaps not forever, but this century will be shaped by one force or the other."

I hugged myself despite the warmth of the leather seat. Whatever the outcome, I told myself, it wasn't my responsibility. I had to make a good decision for myself. And Dorian's hand-picked friends were one thing, but I'd seen plenty of Adelphoi who frightened me every bit as much as Cosimo and Lucretia did—perhaps more.

"You're important to us," Dorian continued, his piercing eyes fixed on me. "I know it's hard for you to believe how important symbols are to agnates."

"To us," I repeated. "To you, as an Adelphoi."

"To me, as myself, as well. I have never hidden how I feel from you, Cora."

No, he certainly hadn't.

He reached across to stroke my cheek. My skin heated at his touch, and I leaned into his hand reflexively.

"You looked so small and sad and so terribly young all alone in that bed when you first woke from your conversion." His voice was a low murmur, and it sent little prickles of awareness down my spine. "And so alive. Like holding fire in my hands. I could hardly remember such a feeling, and it went to my head like a madness. I didn't want to frighten you. I almost frightened myself."

"It was the bond," I protested automatically.

He caught my chin, tilted it so he could look directly into my eyes. "It was you. It was always you."

And then he kissed me for a very long time, and I clung to him as my body answered to his demand, need pooling low inside me until I throbbed between my legs, chafing against my naked thighs.

Finally, the car stopped, and he pulled back. I looked up, bemused, to discover that we were in front of the W Hotel. Doormen jumped forward to swing the Bentley's doors open. Still drunk on Dorian's kisses, I stepped out onto the sidewalk under the covered awning, feeling heavy and light all at once.

Dorian came around to my side and offered his hand. I took it, leaning slightly into his strength, wanting him against me.

"A hotel?" I asked him. His own house in Georgetown could be no more than twenty minutes away.

"You will see," was his only reply.

The doormen swung the doors open, and Dorian led me through into the lobby. I halted just inside, blinking.

"This doesn't seem much like your kind of place," I remarked, surveying the flashy modern space. Black chairs and bright red sofas were arranged on a self-consciously contemporary black and cream rug. Through an arcade was the reception area, a row of lighted white plastic and Lucite desks against a black wall and checkered floor. It seemed far more like Cosimo's scene than Dorian's taste.

"We're not here for the lobby," he said.

Dorian led me past reception with a wave at one of the staff, who nodded, and over to a bank of elevators. We stepped in, and he hit the button for the tenth floor.

"Not the penthouse, then?" I said, trying to provoke some response from him to satisfy my curiosity.

"Not exactly," he said.

The doors opened, and he led me down the hallway, pulling a key card from his pocket. He stopped at a door and opened it.

"Corner suite," he said, flipping on the lights as he stepped into the room. He held the door so that I could pass him. "Though we didn't come for the décor here, either."

I stepped inside and immediately giggled. The

room was extravagant and edgy in a rock star kind of way, all purple and gold. It looked like it belonged on an MTV tour. I started across the dark herringbone wood floor. Then I got a good look out of the bank of windows, and I stopped mid-stride, my jaw dropping.

"Wow," I managed.

"*That's* why we are here. At least partly," he amended.

The hotel towered over its neighbors, the city spreading out beneath us. The room overlooked the long rectangle of the National Mall from one end to the other, and not a single building obstructed the view to the Potomac. The lights glittered across the dark city, as distant and beautiful as stars, and the Washington Monument rose like a white spear over it all.

"Now that's lovely," I said. Impulsively, I went over to the door and turned all the lights off, casting the garish furniture into shadow as the city filled the windows. I sighed.

"So you like it," he said.

"Who wouldn't?" I returned. I pulled off my coat and flopped onto the curved sofa, hurling faux-fur-covered pillows out of my way before toeing my shoes off.

Dorian stepped into the room and crossed to look down at me, his eyes crinkling in amusement. My heart beat a little faster. He was so damnably, sinfully attractive. He hit every button I had without even trying, as if he'd been designed to do just that.

But his smile was touched with more than amusement. That same unreachable sadness lurked there, underneath, a faint echo of old grief.

"What is it?" I asked. I'd seen that look so many times, but I'd never dared to ask before. "What is it that makes you so sad when you look at me?"

He shook his head and swung my feet off the sofa for a moment to sit, replacing them in his lap. He began to work against the arch of one foot with the pad of his thumb through my stocking, and the tension in my muscles flowed out, replaced with delicious awareness of his hands and body.

"Age," he said finally. "Just age. I can't help but think that this is, after all, only a moment, and it will soon be over, like every other moment that has come and gone."

"You said we will have plenty of time," I said, feeling suddenly cold. "Plenty of time for anything."

His hands moved to my other foot, continuing their work. "And we will, until the day the time is all used up."

"There have been others," I said. "Before me, I mean. You've had other cognates." He'd said as much, but I'd never stopped to really consider it, too wrapped up in the here-and-now to give much thought to Dorian's past.

"Yes." His voice was heavy, and he kept his gaze fixed to his hands on my feet as they went still.

"Did you love them?" I asked softly. I didn't know how I felt about it, sharing Dorian with the memories of long-dead women. Which was ridiculous, because I hadn't even decided that I wanted him at all.

Hadn't I?

His shadowed eyes met mine, and now the pain was naked on his face. "Every bit as much as I love you."

The words went through me like a knife, stealing the breath from my lungs as my heart squeezed hard.

He loved me.

He had said so obliquely, telling me that a bond required love, or that it engendered it, but never had he directly spoken those words. And, God help me, I believed him.

He loved me. And he had loved them, too. Had they loved him back?

I looked at the beautiful creature holding my foot in his hands. How could they have resisted any more than I could?

"How many? Who were they?" The words slipped out without my bidding.

"Two," he said. "I can remember two. Hawisa was the first. For seven hundred years, we were together—violent times, turbulent times, those were, and for seven hundred years I kept her safe. Until the day I didn't."

"What happened?"

"It was a stupid local squabble. Not even a proper war." Bitterness dripped from every word. "Hawisa was born just before Romulus Augustulus, the last little emperor of Rome, was deposed and the Western empire faded into chaos and dreams."

Dorian continued, "She witnessed the rise of despots and kingdoms and their fall. But in one brief moment of inattention, when I was away on king's business, a neighboring baron of one of our Navarre estates, a man I called ally and friend, tore through our lands and beat down the great gates and murdered her in our bed. By the time the news reached me, she was gone. It was too fast, too brutal for her to survive."

"What did you do?" I asked, hugging myself.

I saw the echoes of Dorian's wrath still etched in his face. "It was a harsher time, and I was a harsher man. The baron and his line are forgotten to history. The graves of his forefathers were obliterated, and every brick and stone of his residence was lifted and carried away, even the foundation filled in." There was no pity in his voice and no regret.

"And the other?" I asked softly. "Was she killed as well?"

"That was Charlotte. A little French vixen, once a pickpocket dying of smallpox. She was always a reckless one, and I am sorry to say that she did it to herself. A fall from a bridge she had no business climbing, if you can believe it." He shook his head, his smile fond but sad. "She had neither Hawisa's nobility nor your strength of spirit."

Yet he loved her, too. I could hear it in his voice, see it in his eyes.

And he loved me for my spirit. I tried that idea out in my head. It felt strange, as if it didn't quite fit there.

I discovered that I wasn't jealous of these ghosts, these other women who had held Dorian's heart so long ago. Instead, I felt ashamed—ashamed of myself and my doubts of Dorian's ability to feel the emotions I had considered so exclusively human. I wondered if I was even capable of the kind of love that would mourn a partner a hundred years after his loss. Given enough time, could I feel that way about anyone—say, Geoff? Could I feel passions so strong they carried across centuries?

I didn't think so. Except, perhaps, with Dorian. If something were to happen to him right now, with the bond between us, I could hardly think what I would do.

"And...children?" I said, as much to interrupt that thought as anything else.

He shook his head, the sadness receding. "You have met Clarissa already. She has too much of her mother in her. If she doesn't find a cognate soon to ground her, I fear she won't last long."

I gaped at him. "She's your daughter? Why didn't you say? Why didn't *she* say?"

"Such relationships mean less after the first century or so," Dorian said. "She still has a filial tenderness, but she has been an adult for a very long time."

"Right," I said, shaking my head in disbelief.

"We aren't like humans," he said. "We don't drop a litter of children over a period of ten or twenty years. One child a decade at most is all we produce."

"Good thing, too, or otherwise we'd be neck-deep in vampires." I wasn't sure where that came from, but somehow, I was able to joke about it now. Maybe it was because the nightmare of a faceless vampire-child had been replaced with the idea of Clarissa. Despite her wild streak, it was hard to hate her.

I thought of my Gramma and the grief she had endured by outliving her only child. The mother of a vampire would almost never be faced with the same pain. And a cognate would never wear herself out, working herself to death as old age crept up on her....

"I'm sorry, Cora." His voice broke into my reverie. "Tonight was supposed to be a celebration. Our celebration. I didn't mean to burden you with my memories."

I met his eyes, with their icy clarity and their murky depths. "Your past isn't a burden to me, Dorian. There's far too much of you that you hold back, away from me. Too much that I don't know."

His hands began moving again, sliding up to massage my calves. "There's too much darkness in the past. It's best not to dwell on it."

"Your past makes you what you are now," I pointed out. "All of it, not just the happy bits."

"And your past, such as it is?" he asked.

I opened my mouth to reject the idea, then closed it. He was right, of course. The picture-perfect future I'd wanted wasn't just for me. It was for my Gramma, who had wanted it for me more than I ever had.

I'd never really missed having a mother or a father, except in an abstract sense, because I didn't know what it was like to have them. Gramma had been the one to care, though she did her best to hide it. I'd shed most of my tears for my mother in my preteen years, when I had believed, with typical eleven-year-old selfishness, that if my mother had lived, she would have understood me in a way Gramma couldn't. But I'd realized the stupidity of that before I'd even graduated high school.

"I'm afraid of failing Gramma," I said then, before I realized that I'd planned to say anything. "I'm afraid that I'll lose her all over again."

Turning from the path I'd been on when Gramma had died seemed like betraying her memory. I was afraid that maybe she wouldn't recognize me anymore, and I'd somehow lose her twice that way. Since she'd died, I'd felt locked to the dream—and only now did I realize why.

"Do you really think so little of her?" Dorian asked gently. "If your happiness and success was her goal, do you really think she would care if it looked different than what she expected?"

I shook my head. Gramma wouldn't understand my connection to Dorian. How could she? I hardly understood it. And if she suspected anything about his age, she certainly wouldn't approve of it, at least at first.

Of course, no merely human disapproval could survive her first meeting with an agnate.

But even without that factor, I believed that she could become used to the idea of my relationship with him once she became convinced that he wasn't setting out to use me and break my heart.

He was handsome, rich, and suave, and he wanted to cherish me forever. And he would effectively protect me from any of the griefs she had suffered. Could I really believe that she would oppose all that?

It wasn't the future she'd imagined for me any more than it was the future that I'd wanted. But it was a future that she would come to accept—one that she might even be proud of.

If it was what I wanted. And I still didn't know whether it was.

"I suppose I have my own ghosts," I admitted.

"Not tonight," Dorian said. "Let them rest for a few hours. They can go back to haunting you in the morning."

And with that, he slid up my body and kissed me.

CHAPTER SIX

His mouth met mine, and I opened to him, leaning back onto the cushions and pulling him with me, on top of me, into the cradle of my arms and thighs. His lips tasted like everything I had ever wanted, his tongue pushing past my lips and teeth, into my mouth, taking me.

The heat roared up at his touch, lancing down between my legs. My body sang for him. I tilted my hips toward him reflexively, the slick silk of the knee-highs sliding against his pants. He was with me in this moment, seeing only me when he broke off to search my face with those burning eyes before kissing me all over again. But I could still feel the sadness in him, in his hands and body and mouth, and I wished that I had the power to drive it away.

His hands tangled in my hair, his elbows on either

side of my head, holding me at the mercy of his mouth. My arms tightening around him, I pulled him to me as I gave him everything—and took from him, too, drinking his adoration as my due.

At this instant, I was his, completely and utterly. And I would make him mine.

After an eternity that wasn't nearly long enough, his hands slid under my skirt, up my legs, ignoring my thigh-highs, clasping my hips with his thumbs, his long fingers curling around to cup the naked flesh of my rear. His mouth moved under my jaw, lingeringly caressing the curve of my neck.

But I wanted more. I took his face in my hands, pulled him away, up to my mouth again, kissing away the sorrows and the memories. I kissed his cheeks, his jaw, his neck, and the strong line of his throat down to the hollows of his collarbone as his hands roved across my body, cradling my butt, sliding over my hips, my belly, loosening my bra and skirt.

Dorian pushed off me long enough to pull the sweater over my head, and my bra came with it. I attacked the buttons of his shirt as he tugged my skirt over my hips, wanting to touch his body as he touched mine. The last button came loose, and I pushed his jacket and shirt off his shoulders as he pulled the cuffs loose. As he dropped the shirt to the side, my hands freed his belt and fly. He stood up and peeled the rest of his clothes off as I rolled down my stockings and tossed them aside.

And then we were naked, me lying on the sofa, him standing over me, his desire as evident in his eyes as it was in the hard cock that stood proud from the nest of curls.

My throat was tight with everything I wanted to say, to do. But I pushed it all down, held out a hand, and spoke lightly. "Don't just stand there."

That pulled a chuckle from him. "I wouldn't dream of it."

He took my hand, and need shot through me at the touch of our fingers, even before I pulled him down on top of me again. My nipples hardened against the bare flesh of his chest. His mouth covered mine as one arm slid under me, wrapped around me to hold me to him. The other hand skated up to find my clitoris.

His mouth was fierce and hungry, perhaps hungrier than it had ever been before, and I felt in him the aching void of loss and fear, the emptiness that only I could fill. Why he felt it so keenly at this moment, I didn't know, but I felt echoes of it in every touch and his need to possess me utterly.

He rolled my clit in his fingers as his mouth worked against my neck, and I panted into his shoulder. One finger dipped lower, between my folds, teasing me. I shuddered against him. It dipped again, pushing deeper, finding the sensitive place and pressing into it in rhythm with his mouth and body. Another finger slid in beside it, his thumb rolling over my clit, holding me, pushing me up toward a climax, and he lifted his head, looking into my face as I rocked at his touch, at his mercy.

"I love you like this," he said, soft but earnest. "I could watch you forever. You're mine, Cora. All mine.

And I will make you come tonight until you weep with the glory of it."

The words filled my ears, my world. I came around him, clasping his hand with the spasms of my body as my head filled with the roaring of my blood. And in the middle of it, he pulled his fingers clear and drove his cock hard into me, filling me with a shattering abruptness and matching the rhythm of my orgasm to send me spiraling into its grasp and out of control until he was the only thing that was real.

Then he slowed enough to allow my body to let go of its peak, and he made love to me slowly, almost worshipfully, and his rhythm became mine, rocking in the grip of deep waves of pleasure. He sent me over again into the hot grip of a climax, and as I was still shaking in the aftermath, he pulled away and urged me to roll over, onto my stomach.

I did without question, without hesitation. He grabbed one of the garish throw pillows from farther up on the sofa and pushed it under my belly, raising my rear into the air. I looked over my shoulder, but he was already kneeling between my thighs.

Dorian started at the sensitive place in the back of my knee, working with lips and tongue and teeth, and he moved up the inside of my thigh to the edge of my opening, which was swollen and needy from everything he'd already done to me that night.

He lingered there as my breath came fast and ragged, the too-tender flesh between my folds begging for his attentions. I tried to wriggle against him, to make him give me what I craved, but a firm hand on my tailbone pinned me in place, and I had to wait for him to choose to pleasure me.

Finally, after an excruciating time, he moved, teasing the bottom of my entrance with his tongue for a long moment before moving up, between my folds. From that angle, he could scarcely graze the top of my opening, but his tongue moved deeper as he slid back again, finally shoving deep between my folds at the lower end again. He kissed it, suckled against it as I bit my lip hard against my whimpers. My clit was aching, begging for the attention of his mouth.

But he moved lower still, kissing the smooth place just below before swiftly circling my anus with his tongue. The shock of it startled a cry from me, and he slid up my body, kissing my buttocks and the small of my back as he moved until he was working against the back of my neck, throbbing for him now from my clit all the way back.

"When will you understand, Cora?" he whispered into my ear. "I want all of you."

His cock pressed against my swollen entrance, and I whimpered, trying to tilt my hips into him. He increased the pressure slowly, filling me gradually, unbearably, inch by inch. His hand slid between my body and the sofa, finding my breast and cupping it for a moment before slowly tightening around the nipple, teasing it with his fingers as he filled me below. Finally, he came to rest against my body, deep inside, and he began to thrust.

I gasped into the couch—this angle was different from anything I had felt before, pushing harder against the deepest place at the end of each stroke. He drove into me, slowly, deeply, moving almost the entire length of himself out and in. My skin prickled, the heat building up in my center, but it was not enough. I reached for a climax, but it was too far.

"More," I begged. "More, now."

And he gave it to me, speeding up, driving harder, his hand releasing my breast and sliding down to find my clitoris and taking it in his skillful fingers and sending me over into the fire. I called out for him, for Dorian, and I felt him come, too, with me, with a shudder and a low sound, before everything was lost in heat for so long that I thought I'd never come out of it again.

Then he rolled off me, getting to his feet as I lay limply upon the couch with the pillow under my stomach. Dorian offered his hand, and still half-dazed, I took it. He pulled me up and kissed my cheeks. I realized they were damp with the tears of my ecstasy.

He'd done it, just as he'd promised he would.

Dorian led me toward the bedroom, then pulled me into his arms and kissed me hard for a long time until I felt his cock, pinned between us, begin to rise and stiffen again with the swift recovery of the vampire.

"Believe it or not, I didn't bring you here for this, either," Dorian said, touching my face with gentle fingers. "Not primarily, at least."

"It would be in rather poor taste." I smiled up at him. I still felt the darkness in him and echoes of his desperate hunger, and I felt that something important was coming soon, maybe something dangerous. But at that moment I felt unaccountably light.

Dorian swore, abruptly and coarsely. I'd never heard him speak like that before.

"You have no idea what you do to me, do you?" he demanded. "I want to take you so many ways...."

My breath caught. He held me in his gaze. "Show me," I whispered.

He pushed me back onto the bed, my knees buckling as my calves hit the mattress. He came down on top of me. His hands were everywhere, his mouth blazing a trail of sensation across my skin. His kisses deepened, little nips that left me breathless before he kissed away the sting. My knees came up around him, clasping him against me as I rocked my hips into his. His hands slid down my legs, grasping my ankles where they hooked behind him.

Dorian broke off, standing at the side of the bed, holding my ankles in his hands.

"I want to watch your eyes as you come," he said. "I want to see it."

I shook my head, afraid, after everything, of that level of intimacy.

But he said, "For me, Cora," and how could I refuse him?

He pulled my legs straight, spreading them until they ached from the stretch. I bit off a groan of pain. I looked into his eyes, and I could see awareness there—that he was hurting me, that he meant to, and then it twisted in my head, turning around into something else. And it still hurt, but now it hurt so good I could hardly breathe with it, and I could feel myself getting wet with it as I sucked in air.

And I gasped as he drove into me, swift and hard, and pleasure roared up around him and around the place deep inside that he thrust against. His hands held tight on my ankles, and he urged them even farther apart until I whimpered desperately, the burn of the muscles and the pleasure of his thrusting tangled together into a single, overwhelming sensation.

And I didn't look away. Dorian was there, watching me, and I looked back over my breasts that quivered with every thrust, my whole body laid out bared to his eyes as he drove me onward. My hands bunched into fists in the bedspread as I struggled to find myself in the middle of it all. But it was too late—I was already falling apart. I screwed my eyes shut as sensation rose around me—

"Look at me," he ordered.

And reflexively, I obeyed, meeting his gaze even as the orgasm came over me, broke me, tore me into a thousand pieces—still I was caught in those icy eyes, and they seemed to fill my world until there was nothing but him, coming with me, and my pain and my pleasure, all jumbled together until I couldn't tell them apart.

Slowly, slowly I came out of the fog and became aware of other things—the bedspread under me, the cool air on my skin, Dorian pulling away, stepping back. Leaving me alone.

I gave a slight shudder and pushed to a sitting position. The faint remaining aches in my legs were already receding.

While it had lasted, that hadn't been a tease or playing at roughness. It had been real pain.

And I'd loved it, because Dorian had made it so. Another line crossed. So why couldn't I summon the terror this once would have caused me?

And why did that frighten me even more?

Dorian caught my chin, tilted it up to catch my lips in a brief kiss. "Come get dressed for dinner," he said.

I nodded, gathering my scattered wits, and began to head back to the living room of the suite, where my clothes had been left scattered on the floor. But he stopped me, opening a closet door and pulling out a long dress in a deep shade of red.

"Jane sent over everything you need," he said.

I shook my head in bemusement. "You really do change for dinner, don't you?"

"It will be worth it," he said. "I promise."

And I knew he could make that promise come true.

I took the dress and the silver shoes that were on the closet floor, then opened drawers until I found one that held a strapless bra and a pair of panties. I took everything and headed into the bathroom, where I discovered an array of cosmetics and hair products and tools laid out for my use.

I stared at them rather helplessly—I could not hope to replicate Jane's magic. But I cleaned up quickly, pulled on the new clothes, and did my best to repair the damage to my makeup without trying to start from scratch. My hair was hopeless, the finger-waves an impossible mess. I brushed it out and put it in a sleek French twist rather than trying to mimic the artistic disarray that Jane had managed on the night of my Lesser Introduction. I straightened the teardrop necklace self-consciously against my chest, the one Dorian had given me. It caught the color of the dress and seemed to intensify it. I had not taken it off since my date with Geoff.

I stepped out of the bathroom to find Dorian already dressed, dazzling in a tuxedo and black tie. He smiled down at me as he went into the bathroom, and my breath caught a bit despite myself. I simply could not get used to how handsome he was—or how he looked at me.

"Are you ready to go?" he asked.

"I would ask where, but you'd just tell me, 'You'll see,'" I said.

"You know me so well," he replied, his lips twitching.

But did I? I wondered. Every day, there was some new surprise to him, some hidden depth that I hadn't perceived before. Even if I lived to be a thousand, would I ever fully know him?

And would knowing him be worth everything I stood to lose?

CHAPTER SEVEN

He guided me out of the suite and back to the elevator, but instead of hitting the button for the lobby, he hit the top floor—"P.O.V. Lounge," a small sign next to it read.

"So that's the surprise?" I asked.

"The best view in Washington, D.C.," he said. "And tonight, it's all ours."

The doors opened, and Dorian led me out into a dimly lit room scattered with clutches of outrageous furniture in front of a great bank of wide windows overlooking the Capitol and the monuments. It looked like a child's model, as if I could reach out and pluck up the White House for my own amusement.

He was right. The view put even that of our suite

to shame.

For a moment, I thought the lounge was empty. Then I saw the bartender and, over in a corner, a man behind a piano and a full-figured woman in front of a microphone. The pianist was playing softly, and as we moved into the room, the woman began to sing a slow, bluesy song.

"Impressive," I said, trying to compute how much this must have cost him. I decided on far, far too much as he guided me to a pair of red leather loveseats that faced each other across a low cube-style coffee table. I came with him hesitantly, half frightened by the extravagance of it—frightened by what it might mean. Dorian never did anything without a reason.

As soon as we sat, a server materialized with an array of appetizers and took our cocktail orders. The tantalizing smell hit me, and I realized how hungry I was despite the food I'd eaten on the boat. I dug in shamelessly.

Dorian chose some kind of delicate seafood spring roll, then sat back and watched me. The sense of restlessness I had felt from him that afternoon was back, a sort of pent-up energy that seethed beneath his marble composure.

"Do you like it?" he asked, his wave encompassing the lounge, the hotel, everything. I felt like the answer was important to him, deeply important, though I couldn't guess why.

"Of course I do," I said. "Very impressive. Beautiful," I added when that didn't seem like enough. "But you don't have to do something like this for me."

"What's the point of having money if I don't spend it on what I want?" he returned. "It makes me happy to use it this way."

"I don't want to owe you any more than I already do." I owed him my life. How could I even begin to even that score?

"You can't keep accounts for this, Cora," Dorian said, a quiet intensity in his words. "Matters of the heart cannot be drawn up on ledgers."

I shrugged helplessly. I had little in the world beyond myself, nothing to offer him except what I was most afraid to give. And that was exactly what he wanted from me. I couldn't say it was impossible anymore because nothing was impossible with him.

Restively, Dorian pulled his phone from his pocket and glanced at it. "It's almost midnight," he said, sliding it back again.

Midnight. The beginning of a new year. It was less than two weeks ago that I had finished my finals and stepped out of Dorian's Bentley, afraid I would never see another dawn, much less a new year. So much had changed since then—my whole world had turned upside down.

Dorian had changed it all.

I looked across the table at him. If I broke the bond, would I be filled with regret or relief? I would hurt him. I knew it. The sadness I saw in his eyes when he talked about his other cognates, gone so long ago, would include me, too—perhaps a deeper wound, since my separation from him would be from betrayal. At that moment, I felt his future pain as if it was my own.

And I was frightened that I loved him, that I really loved him, both through and beyond the bond that held us. I was afraid that I loved him for who he was, not just what he had done to me. It seemed more and more impossible with every passing moment that what I felt could be nothing but an imposition from something outside of myself—or that it could be removed without taking a piece of me with it.

"Thank you," I said, dropping my eyes to my drink. "I don't think I ever told you that. Thank you for saving me."

No matter what the future held, I was glad to be alive. I hadn't always felt that way since I'd woken. At times I had wondered if I had entered the proverbial fate worse than death.

But now I was glad for it, for everything that had passed between us, even the things that still made my heart shudder in fear. I felt myself slipping closer to that edge, the one from which there was no return.

I still had a choice tonight. I wasn't sure that I would by tomorrow.

"You are more than welcome, Cora," Dorian said. "And that's some part of why I've brought you here tonight—to celebrate your life. Though I understand that it has not entirely worked out as you anticipated."

"That's an understatement," I agreed with a wry smile.

He took a drink of his cocktail, then set it deliberately on the small cube table between us. Again, I had the sense of urges and desires scarcely contained, but when he spoke, his words were measured, almost impersonal. "I have asked—will continue to ask a great deal of you. The world that you have stumbled into is one of the highest stakes, not just for you personally but for all humanity."

I nodded mutely. I refused to accept responsibility for it, but that didn't keep it from being true.

"You see yourself as a victim of circumstance. But my own role was in many ways thrust upon me as well," he said, as if he were weighing every word. "To stay true to what I believed, I was forced into opposition to those who would want to destroy it. Nothing would please me more than to achieve the ultimate goal of my research and retire from society. But I won't be left alone to do that—*we* won't be left alone. We're a part of the world whether we like it or not."

And his sense of duty kept him from even trying. But I didn't have a duty to his world—or to humanity, in the abstract. I'd been just a regular girl, with ordinary dreams.

But I wasn't sure they were enough anymore for the girl I was becoming.

"I just don't know where I fit into that. How I can fit into that. There doesn't seem to be room for *me*," I tried to explain.

He reached across the table and put his hand over mine, sending the familiar, sweet, trembling awareness through me. He threaded his fingers between mine, trapping them as his thumb stroked the palm of my hand, the darkness pulsing with energy within him as it yearned to break free. "All you see are the requirements. There is power, too—in wealth, in the position that I hold in society."

I remembered the guests who had streamed onto Dorian's yacht—senators and lobbyists, he'd said.

"But it's really your power, not mine," I said.

He raised my hand to his lips, kissing each knuckle in turn. My skin came alive in the wake of his mouth, and I shivered.

"Who cares how you come by it?" he murmured against my skin. "Don't underestimate what you can do with it."

"I think you may be overestimating me."

"Never."

Just then, a movement outside of the window caught my eye, and I turned to see the first burst of fireworks rising up out of the Potomac over the National Mall.

It was midnight.

Dorian continued, "You might not have been born for this, Cora. But you were made for it. Just because I'm offering something different than how you imagined your life would be doesn't mean that I'm not offering something more."

"This," I provided, motioning to the empty lounge, the city, and the fireworks beyond.

"Not just wealth, Cora," he said. "Not just an extended life, though I have given you that, too. I offer you meaning. A purpose. A significance that can live on long after we're gone."

It isn't my fight, I wanted to say as I watched his thumb play across the back of my hand. But was it true? If it was a fight for all humanity, then was there anyone whose fight that it wasn't, whether or not I chose to run away?

I hadn't ever looked for meaning in my life. Not like that. And I wasn't sure if I wanted it.

"And I offer you myself."

My eyes snapped to his face, and I caught my breath at the intensity in his icy blue gaze. It cut right through me, into my very core, and I hurt with it.

God, but he was so beautiful in his inhuman perfection, his alien strength. I could feel the force of his will curling around me, roiling in turmoil even as it scarcely brushed my nerves and mind. It was such a part of his presence that I hardly took note of it anymore, but I could feel it now, pulsing with the strength of his desire…for me. For me to choose him. Forever.

The desire that he held back from touching me. Changing me.

"Dorian," I said, and then I stopped. I didn't know what I could say.

He continued, every word fervent. "I offer you everything that I am. I offer you my black soul, for whatever it's worth in this world. I love you, Cora Shaw. My heart is a small thing compared to the destiny of nations, but it is yours."

The weight of the moment hung around my neck like a great stone. I knew that if I took a step, there would be no coming back—not because of him but because of me. I had the sudden sense of standing at the edge of an abyss and looking down, down into eternity….

He offered so much more than I'd ever dreamed of

calling mine. But could it be enough, when my soul was in the balance?

"I—I just don't know," I said.

"You do," he said. "Look inside yourself."

But I already was. I'd been trapped inside my own head for months now, ever since the day of my cancer diagnosis. And what I wanted, really wanted was the impossible. I wanted him and I wanted my old life. I wanted his touch and my small dreams. I wanted everything he offered, and I wanted to always be the same.

"What if I can't do it? What if I can't...." I trailed off, not wanting to say the words.

His hand tightened over mine infinitesimally. "You can," he said. "You must."

And I looked straight into those eyes and into the well of pain, and I realized that he wasn't speaking of forcing me, because the darkness pulsing around him still hardly brushed against the edges of my mind. His words came from his deepest desires.

I must—because he couldn't bear it if I didn't.

Dorian was like a blast furnace, and I was a moth. He seemed so cold only because of the fierce self-control that kept him from destroying me in his heat. He'd offered me the world first, his material possessions and a role as a symbol and maybe even a hero, not because he didn't care about me but because he counted those things greater than his heart, his love. And I ached with the echoes of his pain that he could not realize that his heart and mine were the only things I could care about.

"My God, Dorian," I managed. Fear and loss battled inside me. The image of Geoff, with his good looks and lopsided grin, was already growing faint in my mind.

"While I've changed much of your life, there is at least one human thing I can give you back," he pressed on.

I stared at him as he dropped to one knee in front of me. Just like the first time we met, I thought, a sudden, eerie sense of déjà vu coming over me, when he had taken the vial of blood from my arm and caught the drop that welled up where the needle had been.

Then I looked down at my hand, still clasped in his, and I realized what he intended to do. Panic came over me, and I felt doors slamming all around me. I opened my mouth to speak, to interrupt him, but no sound came out.

"Cora Ann Shaw," Dorian began, his eyes piercing me, so handsome that my heart hurt to look at him, "would you do me the honor of becoming my wife?"

I gasped even though I'd known the question was coming, my heart squeezing so hard that I rocked forward in my chair. Marriage. Marriage to a man I'd known hardly more than a month.

No, not a man. To Dorian—final, forever, a pledge that could not be broken, the choice irrevocably made.

I would never feel with anyone else what I felt with him—not the passion nor the danger. No one would make me feel as wanted, nor would I ever want someone with the depth I felt for him.

But I would always be a pawn in a greater game. He was a monster with a conscience, and it was only that conscience that could save me—but it was also that conscience that might damn me, if the stakes were high enough. And I would be changed. By him. By his world.

By me, if I took what he was offering.

And still he knelt in front of me, the light of the fireworks flickering across his face.

Waiting for an answer. One that, at that moment, I could not give.

I stood abruptly, the tray on the coffee table jittering as I bumped it with my knees.

"I—" I started, then broke off. "I don't know," I managed. "I can't. I need some time—more time."

I couldn't breathe. I couldn't think. I could give him only one answer while he was there, touching me. He knew that. He had to know that. It wasn't right. It wasn't fair.

And for the first time since he'd changed me, I found the strength to pull away—and he let my hand go, let me slide it from between his own.

He didn't have to. He didn't have to let me do anything. And that was exactly why I needed to escape, get away from his influence where I could think clearly, where I could process what he'd just said.

Where I could make my choice.

I spun away and started toward the door. I heard Dorian behind me, and I turned back to see that he'd taken a step away from the table, after me. If he followed, touched me again, kissed me, even with his will clasped so tightly to him, I would be lost forever. My heart was hammering so loudly in my ears that I couldn't hear my own voice.

"Please—please just stay away," I begged, and I

lifted my skirt with one hand, turned back around, and ran.

I slapped the button for the elevator, and it opened immediately. I pushed inside and hit the button for the tenth floor, leaning against the wall as far from his dark figure as I could be as the door slid silently closed between us.

CHAPTER EIGHT

He knows, I thought, breathing fast, too fast, as I stared at the elevator door. He knew what I'd almost done with Geoff, that I'd almost broken the bond. That I knew that I had a choice.

And he wanted me to give it up. To give myself over without reservation, now and forever. To him.

And I didn't know that I didn't want to.

The elevator doors opened, and I stumbled out, my heart beating against my chest. I took two paces before I stopped helplessly.

What was I going to do now? I didn't have a key to the suite, and my purse was still inside, so I couldn't even call a cab to take me home because I had no way of paying for it when I got there.

I'd turned back to catch the elevator again before the doors closed, whether to go up or down I didn't know, when someone called my name.

"Cora!"

I froze, the familiar voice taking me by surprise. I turned back around reflexively and blinked at the empty elevator alcove.

"Cora!"

Following the voice, I stepped out into the corridor. And I saw him.

"Geoff?" I asked incredulously. "What on earth are you doing here?"

It was definitely him, looking every inch the down-to-earth golden boy that he was in a blue Henley and chinos. He looked, for just an instant, like my savior.

"I heard you were going to be here," he said, stepping toward me. He stopped, gave me a quick surveying look. "Damn, you look awesome. I would have taken you somewhere nicer than the movies if I'd known you'd clean up this good."

"Thanks," I said automatically. "But seriously, why are you here?"

"To rescue you," he said. He grabbed my arm and began hustling me toward my suite. His palm was warm and slightly roughened by his lacrosse calluses. "Wow, that sounded melodramatic, didn't it? But I mean it."

I looked at him again, the edges of my surprise blunted now, and I realized that he seemed somehow less impressive than the place he'd occupied in my mind. Handsome, yes, but ordinary in a way that I wasn't anymore.

We reached the door, and he produced a key and slid it into the lock. To my bewilderment, the light blinked green, and he opened the door. I noticed a bandage taped across the back of his hand as he pushed it open and I stepped past him inside.

"What happened?" I asked, nodding at it as I flipped on the lights.

He glanced at the bandage.

"Oh, that? Nothing," he said dismissively. "Cut myself on my way here."

"How did you know I was here?" I asked. "And how did you get a key? And who told you that I needed rescuing? Not that I do, thank you," I added.

"That guy who talked to me the day I picked you up for our date," he said. "He told me where you'd be, gave me a key."

"Cosimo?" I asked, my breath catching in my throat.

"If that's his name," Geoff said. He was talking too quickly, and his eyes were feverishly bright.

I backed away slowly, but he approached, seeming oblivious to my uneasiness.

"He told me everything, Cora. You don't need to be afraid. I understand," he continued.

"What's 'everything'?" I demanded, but I was afraid that I knew.

"About you being bitten by a vampire, turned into his mind-slave," Geoff said.

"And you believed him," I said. Now I knew something was wrong, because the Geoff I knew would laugh that off as craziness. But this Geoff looked deadly serious.

I remembered the cops who nearly shot me under the thrall of a vampire and looked at the bandage on his hand with sudden clarity. This was bad. Really, really bad.

Geoff was standing between me and the door now, which he'd allowed to swing shut. For the first time, I looked at his height, his size, and I was afraid. There was no way that I could stand up to him. No way that I could defend myself.

If I screamed, would anyone even hear? And if they heard, could they come in time?

I pulled off my heels, first one, then the other, as I continued to back up slowly, clutching them in my hand.

"Of course I believe him, Cora," Geoff said. "But don't be afraid. I can help you get free."

Sex with a human would break the bond, forever. No one ever said the sex had to be consensual....

And Geoff was in Cosimo's thrall. He could be made to do anything.

Cosimo had made him want to rescue me. Probably made him love me, too, with the kind of love only a vampire could engender. I could have my old life back, after all, an even better version of my old life, with a lover—boyfriend, husband, whatever I wanted—who was perfectly and entirely devoted to me. Who would never leave me, who would do anything for me, and who would never, ever make me change.

All I had to do was say yes and go with Geoff right then and ask him to break the bond. There would be no rape then. No violence. I'd be free again, free forever.

And I realized with perfect clarity that I would rather die.

I cast around for anything I could use to defend myself, but all I saw were the tacky throw pillows scattered about the floor where I'd tossed them.

"He cut you, didn't he?" I demanded. "Cosimo, I mean. He had you drink something—"

Geoff made an impatient noise. "None of that matters. I'm here to get you free, Cora. He warned me that the monster might have perverted your mind, but as soon as it's over, you'll see what I've done for you."

"You're talking about rape, Geoff," I said. "Do you understand that?"

He shook his head. "It's not really you who's saying that. He's inside your head, Cora. That's why you rejected me that night."

"The only reason I invited you up at all was because I thought that maybe I wanted to break the bond," I said. "Because it's my decision to make."

But now I was going to lose both the decision and the bond I thought I didn't want. The thought filled me with a choking panic. I was really going to lose Dorian. I wasn't playing with the idea or weighing it—it was going to happen, here and now, whether or not I wanted it to.

And my heart splintered into a thousand tiny pieces.

I'd been so wrong. Wrong to fear the lesser terror. Wrong to run away. And now I'd pay the ultimate price.

There was no reasoning with Geoff now. Not after Cosimo had messed with his head. And I'd begged

Dorian not to follow me....

Geoff came toward me even as I fell back, deeper into the room. "It's the sickness talking, Cora. Come with me, and it'll all be over in just a little while, and then you'll see. I love you so much. All I want is to make you happy—the real you."

I screamed then at the top of my lungs, and I threw the shoes at him. They bounced harmlessly off his chest, his earnest expression showing no reaction at all. He continued to advance as I backed up towards the wet bar.

He isn't Geoff, I told myself. *Not now. Not really.* My groping hand encountered a bottle, and I threw it hard.

He caught it easily and let it drop harmlessly to the floor, where it rolled away.

I screamed again, even louder. *"Help me! Somebody—anybody. Help!"*

"Hush, Cora. I'm not going to hurt you," Geoff said. He was only a few steps away now, still squarely between me and the door. Pinned against the wet bar, I had no place to go.

I reached behind me and began hurling glasses at him. He brushed away the one that would have hit his face and ignored the others, letting them strike his body and shatter on the floor. I found another bottle, swung it—

And Geoff caught my wrist before it could come crashing down on him, plucking the bottle from my grasp and setting it back on the wet bar.

"Be quiet, now," he admonished.

I screamed again, kicking and biting, struggling to

hit or scratch him. But he outweighed me by eighty pounds of muscle, and he deflected or ignored my blows.

Dorian, please! Save me, Dorian. Please! The words were a frantic chant in my mind. I'd told him not to come. I'd told him to leave me alone. I'd stripped myself of my protection, and now my only hope was that he'd listen to my heart as I called for him.

Geoff grabbed for my dress and tore it from my shoulders with one motion, pulling it down to my ankles with one more wrenching yank that nearly knocked me off my feet. He reached for my panties as I struggled against him, his arm pinning me with my back to his chest.

I wasn't even trying to form words anymore, just screaming over and over, the sounds tearing at my throat. He snagged the edge of my panties and pulled hard, the elastic cutting into my flesh as the seam gave. He dropped them and fumbled at his fly. I threw my entire weight to the side, wrenching free with such force that I sprawled against the floor.

Shards of glass from the shattered barware cut into my hands and knees, but I scrambled to my feet and darted around him, running for the door.

Geoff was faster, though, and his body hit me, slamming me into the wall and knocking the wind out of me as lights flashed behind my eyes. I dragged in a breath, trying to clear my vision as I struck out blindly.

"It's all right, Cora," he kept muttering. "It's going to be all right."

His pants were loose around his hips, and he was

pulling out his cock.

This is really going to happen, I thought with frantic clarity. *This is really, really happening, and I can't stop it.*

"Dorian!" I screamed one last time, and then the room exploded.

Dorian came through the door so fast that I hardly saw him, his vampiric will lashing through the room with such force that my vision darkened. And he was the most beautiful thing that I had ever seen in my life.

"Stop!" he ordered, and every muscle in my body went instantly stiff in obedience.

But Geoff was under Cosimo's thrall, impervious to Dorian's control, and he continued to jerk at his clothes, intent on his assault.

Dorian moved faster than any human could, smashing into Geoff and flinging him across the room even as I dropped to the floor hard, my rigid muscles unable to save me.

Dorian raised a fist, and I forced my tongue to work inside my frozen jaw.

"Don't kill him! Don't kill him!" I pleaded. "It was Cosimo. He's done something to him."

Dorian cast me a look, and in it I saw such darkness, such vengeance and black fury that I could taste it in the back of my mouth.

But he stopped—Dorian stopped, and he scooped up one of the glass shards from the ground before stalking forward swiftly as Geoff struggled to his feet. I saw him make two slashing motions—one on his hand, the other on Geoff's. The blood ran free. Dorian clasped their hands together for an instant, palm to palm to make the blood mingle, even as Geoff fought against him. Then there was another movement, almost too fast to follow, he had Geoff in a headlock and was forcing his cut hand against Geoff's mouth.

Geoff sputtered and kicked for an instant, then grew frighteningly slack in Dorian's arms. Disdainfully, the vampire dropped the boy and stepped back.

Geoff lay curled against the floor for a long moment.

Was he—? But just then he stirred, pushing to his hands and knees as he shook his head as if to clear it.

He looked up, first at Dorian, then at me.

"Holy shit. It's true." All the color ran out of Geoff's face, and he stumbled to his feet. "Oh, shit," he repeated. "Shit."

He jerked up his pants, and I saw in his broken face what Cosimo had done to him—what I'd indirectly caused Cosimo to do. If I'd still been capable of feeling anything for him, I would have wept.

"Get. Out." Dorian's words lashed out again, and Geoff, under his control now, jerked like a puppet on strings and fled past me. I would have recoiled if my muscles had been under my control. He was gone in an instant, the door swinging shut behind him.

And all of a sudden, my body went limp, and my brain went blank with relief.

CHAPTER NINE

Dorian was instantly at my side, dropping next to me and saying something low and urgent. My half-stunned mind caught up and processed what it was.

My name. Over and over again, like it was being torn from his very soul, Dorian was saying my name.

I started to push up off the floor, but he grabbed my wrists. I hadn't noticed the blood flowing down them from the slices on my palm, dripping onto the floor. With a hiss, he plucked the fragments of glass from my palms and lifted my hands to his mouth, kissing them over and over again. His face was stricken, lines of the deepest grief carved into the marble of his beauty, and the darkness roiled and pulsed around him.

I only realized then how complete his power was over me. I'd known it, but I hadn't felt it before that moment in which my mind surrendered before his like a moth to a blowtorch. With a word, he had frozen my body. With another, he could freeze my heart.

But he had stopped. When I had called out to him to spare Geoff, he had stopped, even in the heat of a fury so intense that the force of it had filled the room.

He pulled my hands from his mouth and looked down at them. Where he touched me with his mouth, the skin had healed instantly, leaving only a faint tracery beneath the blood.

Dorian clasped my hands in his and closed his eyes and swayed, his breath rasping loudly in his throat.

And then I understood.

"I'm still a cognate," I said numbly. "I'm still yours."

And my heart sang.

I'm his, still his, forever and ever and ever his....

A shard of glass dropped from my knee to the floor. My other wounds were healing, too, though slower without Dorian's touch.

Of course I was his. I knew what had happened—and what hadn't. And I didn't know what a broken bond would feel like, but what pulsed between us now was whole and true and good. But for just an instant, utterly irrationally, I had almost thought the worst.

He opened his eyes then and fixed them on my face, searching it as if he were memorizing every line. "I'd feared—" He broke off, and a shudder went through his frame.

And yet he'd drunk my blood. Drunk it anyway, even though if I had been changed back, he would have died.

Because without me, he didn't want to live.

I looked into those cold blue eyes, so terrible and so haunted. "You let him live. Why? I thought you'd kill him for sure."

He pressed my bloodied hands against his chest. I could feel his heart beating there, too fast and too hard, the heart that he had given me. "You told me not to. And you were right. He was a pawn. He didn't deserve to die."

All the wrath I'd seen, the indescribable fury, had been constrained at my word. The thought shook me, that I had such power over him. It was a power he chose to give me—but perhaps, in its way, it was almost as much power as he held over me.

Dorian scooped me up and carried me into the bedroom as bits of glass fell from my feet. I buried my face against his chest, the first shudders of shock going through me. I breathed him, his scent, as if I would never smell it again, and his arms felt like the only home in the world.

"I felt you," he said. His face was a mask now, but his voice trembled, almost imperceptibly. "I felt your distress, and at first, I thought you were still upset about the proposal. I didn't realize there was something wrong until it was nearly too late. I almost didn't come in time. My God, Cora—" His voice broke. "I almost lost you."

I tightened my arms convulsively around his neck as he carried me toward the bathroom. My naked flesh was smeared with my blood, staining the satin of my strapless bra and the snowy expanse of his tuxedo shirt. "It wasn't your fault." The words came from me but as if they were very far away. "I told you to stay away."

"All that matters is that I nearly failed." All his seething darkness turned inward in anger and guilt.

Everything felt so unreal. I knew it would hit me any moment, what had happened—and what had almost happened. Right now, though, I felt like I was floating in a kind of waking dream. "No. All that matters is that you succeeded. Cosimo tried to take me away from you, but you stopped him."

Dorian stopped mid-step. "You know it was him?"

"Yes," I said. "Geoff—that's the boy, he's my friend or was my friend or—" I shook my head. All that was irrelevant now. "He described him to me before, hanging around my apartment, and I'm sure it was Cosimo."

Dorian started again, passing through the bathroom door.

"He will be dealt with."

Bending, he laid me in the half-egg of the freestanding tub. My bloodied feet left shocking red smears on the white acrylic as I curled them under me. Dorian set the temperature and turned on the tap, and hot water poured into the tub, sending billows of steam up into the room. It turned faintly pink when it touched my skin, washing the blood away. I was trembling despite the heat of the water. Dorian touched my shoulder with his hand lightly, reassuringly.

"You're safe now, Cora. I will be right back," he

said. He stepped out of the room, shutting the door behind him.

The water felt like the first real thing that had happened since Dorian burst into the room, tickling at my feet and knees, the heat of it melting my frozen shock. I hunched over, hugging myself, and with the abruptness of the tap turning on, I started to cry.

I cried at what had just happened, what had been done to me and what had been done to Geoff because of me. I cried for everything I had lost—my Gramma, my humanity, my innocence, my youth. And I cried for the future, so dangerous and terrifying, and about the vampire who scared me as badly as anyone ever had but whom I couldn't live without.

Because I knew that truth now as absolutely as I had ever known anything.

The water rose up around me, lapping at my thighs and then my belly. And all I could do was surrender myself to the sobs.

The thought that I was going to be severed from Dorian forever frightened me worse than the violence of Geoff's assault, because a rape I might survive. But losing Dorian—that was beyond bearing. After all those weeks and months of being strong, of bearing up, of facing down impossible odds…that was the loss that would have broken me.

I had to choose. There was no in between with Dorian. It was all or nothing.

And while my mind had hesitated, my heart had chosen Dorian. No matter what the cost.

The door opened. I heard it, but I was crying too

hard to even look up. Suddenly, Dorian was there, stepping into the tub as the water soaked his tuxedo pants and Italian leather shoes. The water sloshed as he eased down behind me, and then he pulled my almost-naked body against his chest.

My hands fisted around the cloth of his jacket as if I were still afraid he'd disappear, clinging to him, afraid of him but even more afraid of losing him.

The water rose, creeping up our bellies to our chests. I cried and hiccoughed against the strength of his chest, against the cotton of his shirt stained with my blood and tears and darkened with water that crept up toward the edge of the tub.

His arms encircled me, cradling me against him like a child as he kissed the top of my head, murmuring softly, constantly. Most of the words I didn't understand, spoken in languages I'd never heard and perhaps no living human knew any longer. But the ones I did understand only made me cry harder.

"Hush, my love. It will be all right. My love, my life, my heart, my soul, you will see, you will see…."

I didn't know how long it was until I stopped, but Dorian had to reach around me and turn off the tap, and the water had turned tepid by the time I washed the last of the snot and the tears from my face, my soul wrung out and emptied.

I looked up at him. I should have been ashamed for him to see me like this, ashamed of anyone witnessing the ugly depths of my self-pity and grief. But I wasn't. I couldn't be. Not with him.

My vampire.

I knew what I had to do. What I wanted to do, if only because the alternative was unthinkable.

"The answer is yes," I said, my voice ragged, shaking from my tears.

His eyes widened, and I realized that, for once, I had shocked the unflappable Dorian Thorne.

"Yes," I repeated, my heart beating so hard that it thundered in my ears. "Dorian Thorne, I will marry you."

Speechless for the first time since I had met him, he tilted my chin up with a finger hooked beneath my chin, and he kissed me.

Reaction roared through every nerve at his touch, fierce and triumphant, and I met his gentle kiss with all the desperation of my fear. I kissed him hard, my hands in his hair, dragging his mouth down to mine. I tasted him, drank him, as if I could take his essence into myself.

If I was his, then I would make him mine.

I twisted so that I could kiss his cheeks, his jaw, his strong throat, moving fast, my kisses rough with urgency. I wanted him with me, in me, taking me forever, so I didn't even have to think of losing him again.

I reached under the water and found the edge of his cummerbund where it met his pants. I could feel the hard bulge through the fabric. Slipping my hands under it, I found the button of his fly and pulled it loose, my hands fumbling with hurry. I needed him more than I had ever needed anything. I pulled the zipper down and slid my hand in, finding the slit in his underwear and the hard flesh beneath.

He made a low sound in his throat as my hand encircled him, and he caught my wrist, holding my hand in place as I worked my mouth against his neck.

"Cora, you don't have to—"

I broke off from kissing him to interrupt. "Yes, I do. Right now. I almost—" I cut myself off. I'd almost lost him. Lost this. "Let me do this, Dorian."

And he closed his eyes, his face pinched with a flood of emotion I could almost taste. But all he said was my name: *"Cora."*

Taking it for permission, I turned in his lap, hooking my legs over his to straddle him. He opened his eyes, and there was an intensity there that was a reflection of my need. He found the back of my bra and unfastened it with a twist, dropping it to float free. Pushing me up with his knees under my rear as the water sloshed around us, he dipped his head and flattened his palm, holding me against his mouth as it moved down to capture one of my nipples.

It went hard instantly as he took it into his mouth, and I arched back as my body's response jolted up my spine and down between my legs. Wet from the bath, it sealed to his mouth, aching and swelling under the suction as his tongue rasped against it.

I whimpered as he released it, only to take the other one, claiming it as thoroughly, as if he were marking me as his. I stroked his cock to the rhythm of his mouth, and it throbbed in my grasp. My other hand twisted the lapel of his jacket as the need burned through my nerves, up into my skull, where it set up a pounding beat.

He raised his head and I pulled myself toward him, along his legs until my knees met the bottom of the tub and the juncture of my thighs pressed up against my hand that still encircled him. He made a strangled noise between his teeth as my folds came up against his shaft. Desperate to be filled, I lifted up, guiding him inside me as he shifted his grasp to my hips.

I slid down over him, his thickness stretching me and sending a throbbing heat down into me, where he belonged. I grabbed his shoulders and kissed him again, long and hungrily, and his tongue stroked me, invaded my mouth, sending tremors straight down into the place that he filled until I couldn't bear it anymore and I began to move, sliding my body up his length and driving it down again, the water lapping at the edge of the tub with my motions. I rode him, and it was his turn to arch back against the hard rim of the tub, the expression on his beautiful face so intense it almost broke my heart.

The water pushed back, slowing my motions, fighting our bodies until I found a harmony with it. Inside me, pleasure twisted tighter until everything seemed to run together, my body and his and the water around us. Then he reached between us and found my clitoris, and the world broke apart, and I rode the wave until he came in me, under me, in the depths of my orgasm.

I slumped forward against the heat of his chest under his wet shirt, lying there as the waves we'd started in the water bumped against each other and our bodies until the water gradually grew still. He held me to him, and I didn't move even as he grew soft inside me because I never wanted to let him go.

Mine. He belonged to me, heart and dark and tortured soul, every bit as much as I belonged to him.

But time didn't stop for me, and the water slowly leached its heat into the room until goose bumps rose across the parts of my flesh that were not pressed against him.

He gave me a kiss, sweet and slow, and then shifted me off him, to the side, and reached past me to open the drain. He stood, water sheeting from his ruined clothes, and stepped out of the tub. He caught a bath towel from the nearest hook and held out a hand to me, still wordless.

I took it, stepping reluctantly from the bath and back into the world. He wrapped the towel around my body, then caught my face in his hands and kissed me one more time. Then he stepped back and began stripping the soaked clothes from his body. But I stepped up and pushed his hands away and began working down his shirt studs myself, revealing his glorious skin.

Looking down at me, he said, "I didn't want to leave you alone in here, but I had to make arrangements—tell the Adelphoi what happened so they could deal with Cosimo and send for bodyguards, in case another attempt is made. We'll keep you safe."

I shook my head. "Will you? After the djinn in the parking lot, and now this? Even if you get Cosimo, he's one of the Kyrioi. They're in it together, or at least some of them are, and there are others who can come after me. Don't make promises you can't keep."

"You could have gone with him willingly." He looked at me keenly as he freed the last stud on his shirt. "That boy. He was your friend. More than your friend."

"Not anymore," I said through the tightness in my throat. I'd lost Geoff twice in all of this, once through my choice to stay with Dorian and again in what Cosimo and then Dorian had done to him.

"You ran away from me because I frightened you, and yet when he came, you fought him instead of taking what he offered."

"Freedom." I whispered the word.

"Cosimo told you that, didn't he?"

I nodded mutely, pushing his jacket and shirt from his shoulders.

He freed the studs at his wrists and dropped the clothes on the floor with a wet slap. "If you'd gone with him, it would all be over, and you wouldn't have to be afraid anymore."

Each word was distinct, as if he had formed it with the utmost care and spoke it with infinite cost.

I closed my eyes, just for a second. It was true. I could have taken what Geoff offered, regardless of the reason, and I'd be free now. Free—and bereft. The price was far too high. I met the pain in Dorian's eyes. "I don't want to be safe if it means I can't be with you. I love you. I may be crazy, but I do."

"I know," he said quietly. "I just wasn't certain that you did."

I stood there, rooted to the cold tile. "Never let me go. Promise me that—that you'll never let anyone take me from you again."

His step caught me against his naked chest. "Not even you?" he asked.

"Especially not me," I whispered. "I'm so scared."

"I know that, too. But you're far braver than you think."

I laughed unsteadily. "I hope so. Otherwise, I don't think I can bear it."

"I know you can, because I know how I feel for you. And my love would bear me over mountains, across deserts, and through the gates of hell itself. If you feel even the faintest echo of that, you are strong enough for anything."

I looked into his blue eyes, burning with an icy fire, and I knew that every word he spoke was true. He loved me like no one else would—like no one else could.

To the ends of the earth.

No matter what the cost.

CHAPTER TEN

I sat on the bed, wrapped in the towel, as Dorian dressed in the pants he'd worn to the yacht party a few hours and a lifetime before. He stepped out of the bedroom, and I stiffened as I heard voices in the next room.

The bodyguards, I realized, relaxing. Just as he'd said. They were here to protect us—to protect me.

He came back in, carrying my duffel bag and a Louis Vuitton train case. He set the train case on one side of the bed and brought the duffel bag to my side.

"You'll find night clothes and the rest of your toiletries in there," he said. He stripped off the pants and traded them for a pair of loose pajama bottoms from his suitcase.

Pajamas on a vampire, I managed to think despite everything. That was not something you saw every day.

"We're staying here tonight?" I rummaged in the duffel bag. Sure enough, my own t-shirt and undies were there. I dropped the towel and pulled them on. "Are you sure it's safe? The Kyrioi know we're here."

He walked over to stand between my knees, bending down to kiss my forehead. I sighed and leaned into his caress.

"It's safer than moving, with the force that's stationed outside that door, and the Kyrioi have other things to worry about tonight."

Whoever he'd sent after them, he meant. I nodded. "Who's out there?"

The corner of his lip twitched. "More than a dozen men—mine and some reliable contractors."

I started to ask about how he'd gotten the hotel staff to agree to so many in the room—and then shut my mouth. Of course the staff would agree. When agnates make a request, who says no?

"We have lookouts downstairs in the lobby, as well," Dorian continued. "And tomorrow, you and I will take the yacht for a trip as soon as the last party guest is ejected and the boat cleaned and restocked."

"A trip? Where?" I frowned, shaking my head. That wasn't the question I should be asking. "I mean, don't you think you should ask me first?"

He stopped, blinked, and said, "Did I not? I believe that you'll be safest on a boat while my allies deal with the Kyrioi. Djinn are no worry when you're surrounded by saltwater, and neither are humans who might try to press unwanted attentions on you. Will you come?"

"What about school?" I asked.

"The first day of classes is still more than twenty days away. My allies will deal with the Cosimo problem while you are safely out of the crossfire during that time." He paused and raised a sardonic eyebrow. "Or does the idea of two weeks or so in the Caribbean with me really seem that abhorrent to you?"

"Of course not. I just prefer that you ask—and keep me up to date." I took a deep breath. All of this seemed impossible and strange. "But I'll go. Since you're asking me, I'll go."

He smoothed my damp hair away from my face. "By the time you get back, you won't have to fear a single human's attack any longer."

"Because I'll change more," I said, remembering what Clarissa had said. "When does all the changing stop? Will I still be...me then?"

He pulled me to my feet, into his arms. "Don't be afraid, Cora. You'll still be the same person. Only stronger on the outside, as you already are on the inside."

"Stronger, faster, prettier—better," I said, filling in the word. It was really going to happen, all the changes that I'd feared. I had chosen them.

"No," he said. "You are perfect as you are."

I shook my head.

He tilted up my chin. "Yes, Cora. You are perfect to me. Now and always."

He kissed me then, and the world slid out of focus for several long minutes as I gave myself up to him and

110

the reassurance of his touch, his body, his love.

Finally, he broke away with a sigh. "Tomorrow, we'll visit my jeweler while the yacht is being prepared for us to leave."

"Jeweler?" I echoed.

His lips twitched. "For a ring."

"Oh." The engagement ring. The thought still filled my stomach with butterflies, objections crowding again in my mind. I was too young. I hardly knew him. I would give up so much....

But I would gain him. And that was worth everything in trade.

I took a deep breath.

"You really are serious about it, aren't you? The whole wedding thing."

"Completely," he said.

I stood there with his arms around me, and I thought about what it would mean—a cognate who had been screened for compatibility and who had chosen to risk death in return for a chance at life who chose again to unite with him in a human ceremony.

"It's about more than me, isn't it?" I said. It wasn't really a question. "It's about your cause. Our wedding would be a triumph for the Adelphoi."

"It is about you. But yes, it would be a triumph for us," he corrected.

My hand was on his chest. I turned it so that I could see the bond-mark there, on my wrist. Our cause. I wasn't ready to go that far. Not yet. I wasn't any kind of activist, any sort of hero.

But I was willing to do it for him—make the wedding into everything it could be.

"All right," I said. "We'll give them something to talk about."

"Let's get to bed, then," he said, smoothing my wet hair away from my face. "It will be a long day tomorrow."

I looked up into those light blue eyes. "Only if you hold me tonight."

In answer, he sat down on the bed and gathered me instantly into his arms. "Every night, Cora. Every single night."

CHAPTER ELEVEN

I woke up to Dorian's kiss on my cheek. I turned to catch his mouth, sleepily pulling him toward me.

He gave a deep, rich chuckle that thrilled through me and pulled back to stand beside the bed. "It's breakfast time. Then we need to go."

Those words brought me back to myself—brought back everything that had happened the night before. The proposal. Geoff. My acceptance.

I looked up at the beautiful creature who was to be my husband. From his dead-black hair to his flawless features to his pale eyes, he seemed to be constructed to play on every ideal of human desirability.

He was mine. As I was his.

The idea thrilled and frightened me. And I couldn't

regret a thing.

I took in the suit he was already wearing and sighed at the necessity of getting dressed.

"Let's go, then," I said, extending him a hand to help me drag myself out of bed.

Once dressed, I stepped into the living room of the suite like a newborn fawn on unsteady legs. I'd made my choice. My happily-ever-after had come, and I was on the other side of it and surprised by it all the same. I'd thought of my choice almost as if it would be the final chapter in my life, but I realized that it was just the beginning of something new.

The living room had been cleaned up, every trace of glass and blood now gone. I kept my gaze averted from the empty places above the wet bar where the wineglasses that I had thrown had been.

Men and women stood at a kind of parade rest around the circumference of the room, at least a dozen of them. My skin prickled under their eyes. Men and women, yes, but not ordinary ones. I couldn't get a sense of what all of them were, but at least three were djinn, and some others were…werewolves? When I looked past them or saw them out of the corner of my eye, it was like I could see them double, one version human, the other animal.

Dorian caught me staring warily at them.

"Mercenaries work for every side," he said shortly.

"Are they loyal?" I asked—which was probably less than polite, but my previous experiences with the golden-eyed djinn had not been good.

"Elizabeth trusts them," Dorian said.

That wasn't really an answer at all, and at my look, he gave me a half-shrug.

An enormous spread of food was laid out on the coffee table, as if its sheer extravagance could somehow strike back against the dangers of the night before. I hadn't finished dinner, and my stomach rumbled loudly at the sight, eliciting a smile from Dorian. I piled a plate full and ate with a will. Dorian filled a smaller plate and sat next to me on the couch. I slid over so that our thighs touched, needing the reassurance of the contact.

"So you have a jeweler," I said when I had slowed down enough to talk.

"Of course," he said.

Right. Of course. What man doesn't have a jeweler?

"Do you often shower women with necklaces and rings, then?" I prompted.

He chuckled and raised his hands, his wrists facing me. I stared at them blankly.

"Cufflinks, Cora," he said. "Shirt studs and tie clips. And watches, too, though I don't often bother with them anymore."

"Oh," I said, feeling a little silly. I hadn't really thought of where those things might come from.

"And, yes, also women's pieces," he said. "Even an agnatic woman is still a woman, and some have heads that are turned by such things."

"For your politics," I said.

He nodded. "If you would like to be included in our discussions in the future, it is your choice."

My choice—only because he gave it to me. Because

it was, ultimately, Dorian's decision, not mine. As everything in my life would be from this point onwards.

I took a steadying breath. I trusted him. I did—I trusted him with my life because I didn't think I could trust myself with it. But I'd grown up in a world where I'd believed in equality in relationships, and ours could never be equal.

Aloud, I said, "Thanks. I might at some point. Right now, I think I just want to get through the next semester in one piece. And our wedding," I added.

"As you wish," he murmured.

And it would be. I was convinced of that. I just didn't know what it was that I would wish in ten years, much less twenty or thirty. I put my free hand over my midsection. By then I might have children.

Oh, God, and if I did, I must be sure that those children would be free from the burden of causing another's death....

After breakfast, one of the mercenaries brought our outerwear, and I shrugged into my coat somewhat awkwardly as it was held by a musclebound hulk who managed to make even Dorian seem slender. Other mercenaries took up our luggage, and the rest surrounded us, hustling us through the lobby and out the front door to Dorian's Bentley, waiting at the curb. One of them got in the front passenger seat as we got in the back. The others piled into other cars that were almost aggressive in their nondescriptiveness.

I wondered what the chauffeur made of all this, but if he thought anything at all, I couldn't tell. I threaded my fingers through Dorian's, holding onto them a little too hard.

And my heart was glad. Even as my head feared for my future, my heart shed its last doubts. I looked over at him as he watched the streets slide by outside the window, and I thought *I love you* with so much force that it almost hurt.

The chauffeur dropped us off in front of an unassuming shop in Old Town Alexandria. "King's Jewelry," read the white words on the black awning above. The mercenaries joined us on the curb and fanned out around us as Dorian pulled me under the shelter of his arm. We walked into the store, and immediately, a sales associate ushered us through the showroom and into the back.

The room there was dark and so small that only four guards followed us in, standing up against the wall. Across from us was a solid wall made of shallow metal drawers, hundreds of them, and in front of that was a velvet-covered table with the jeweler hovering to the side.

Dorian pulled out the single chair for me, and I sat, facing the table, and caught my breath as I looked down. Tray after tray of rings and loose diamonds lay there, a hard light shining down on them from above so that they glittered, dazzling me.

There were thousands of them. There had to be. Some rings had diamonds so small that I could hardly make out the individual stones, while others were the size of a chunky pebble.

"Whatever you wish," Dorian said, waving at them.

I reached forward. They were beautiful, stunning in

their purity. Hesitantly, I tilted the trays in turn so that I could see them more clearly, more than half afraid to touch them.

They were all so bright and clear, so direct in their beauty. I looked up at Dorian, who was anything but.

"What is it, Cora?" Dorian asked as the jeweler hovered in the shadows.

His expression was unreadable, as it so often was, and with his aristocratic looks, it made him seem as distant as the moon, far beyond my reach. But despite that, he belonged to me, as much as such a creature could belong to anyone.

"The diamonds," I said. "They aren't right."

He raised an eyebrow. "What would be right?"

I shook my head. I didn't know.

With a sharp nod, Dorian took the jeweler aside for a moment, murmuring something to him. The man whisked the trays of diamonds from the table, sliding them back into the drawers that lined the room. I gave Dorian a questioning look, but the only reaction he gave was the arching of a brow, so I settled back to wait.

The jeweler busied himself in his cabinets for several minutes before returning to the table with a tall stack of trays, which he began to set before me.

No longer was there an endless parade of diamonds—now precious stones of every type were laid out before me, rubies and sapphires, peridot and citrine, even pearls and amber and other things I couldn't name.

My gaze was drawn by one tray, full of smooth, black stones that glinted with blue and green and fiery red, flecks of color the seemed to be lighted from within.

The darkness and the fire.

"Ah, black opals," the jeweler said as I picked one up. "An elegant stone. Opals love to be worn, as the skin keeps them strong. If they are stored away too long, they can become dry and brittle and will shatter at the least touch."

Some were so dark they were almost muddy. Others were a chaotic wash of color. I picked through the tray until I found one that was perfect—though it had a base of the deepest black, it glowed flame-red and blue and green with the strength of the color within.

"This one," I said, looking up at Dorian.

His expression unreadable, he said, "As you wish."

After that it was a matter of sketching out an appropriate setting, which the jeweler did with swift skill. I approved it, handing the stone over to him reluctantly, and we left, Dorian pausing to kiss me again just inside the door.

I would never get tired of his touch.

"I can't even put into words—" He broke off, shaking his head, and kissed me again. My Dorian, for once was speechless.

Real. It was all impossibly real and permanent—the bond, Dorian, everything. I thought I should be able to float up to the sky, I felt so light to have the burden of it lifted from my shoulders. In the car, I pulled out my phone and typed out a quick email:

Hey, everybody! I'm going to be out of range for a while— taking an unexpected trip out of the country, and I don't think I'll have phone or internet access. I'll see you all when school starts, if not before. Hugs, Cora

I scrolled through the list of email addresses, adding all my college friends. My finger hesitated over Geoff's name. Biting my lip, I added him, too.

The yacht was waiting for us in its slip, all traces of the New Year's Eve party swept away. We left our guards on the pier and took the gangway up to the boat.

I stood on the deck, facing the docks, as the yacht began to pull away. Slowly, we moved down the Potomac, the capital slipping away before me, foot by foot.

"We'll be back." Dorian's voice was a rumble as I leaned against him, his arms crossing my chest to hug my body against his.

I tilted my head to look at him. His eyes were fixed on me.

"I know," I said.

We'd be back, but it wouldn't be the same. I was leaving a life in College Park, a life of classes and friends and a familiar, carefully rehearsed future. When I came back, it would not have changed. But I had. I wouldn't be able to fit in it anymore. My world was too big now.

My world, which now centered around Dorian. The flame to my moth. Darkness, shot through with the most beautiful light, one I could not tear myself away from.

My hands tightened on his wrists as I turned back toward the shore, watching it all slip away, behind us.

I loved him, this creature suspended between good and evil. My fallen angel, my rising demon.

And whatever the price, I could never let him go.

The story continues in…

For All Time

Cora's Bond – Book 1

Aethereal Bonds

Want to read the first chapter right now? Sign up for the newsletter at AetherealBonds.com to get exclusive access—for free! Get free content and release updates.

Dorian Thorne and Cora Shaw return from their Caribbean and plunge into the thick of vampiric politics—and Cora is caught right in the middle. She is determined to manage her relationship with Dorian, their wedding plans, and her final semester of college.

But there are factions in deadly opposition to their wedding, and as events begin to unfold, it appears that there is more on the line than either of them suppose.

About the Author

V. M. Black is the creator of Aethereal Bonds, a sensual paranormal romance urban fantasy series that takes vampires, shifters, and faes where they've never been before. You can find her on AetherealBonds.com. Visit to connect through her mailing list and various social media platforms across the web.

She's a proud geek who lives near Washington, D.C., with her family, and she loves fantasy, romance, science fiction, and historical fiction.

All of her books are available in a number of digital formats. Don't have an e-reader? No problem! You can download free reading apps made by every major retailer from your phone or tablet's app store and carry your books with you wherever you go.

Made in the USA
Lexington, KY
04 January 2015